Vikram and Vetāla

Praise for *Vikram and Vetāla*

'A fascinating retelling of the ancient story cycle of the *Baitâl Pachchisi* … Penick is an unusual and extraordinary scholar.'

—Namita Gokhale, from the Introduction

'These ancient fables skim the surface of characters and places, blurring into one another as they accumulate a repetition of lustful monarchs, forlorn princesses, handsome Brahmins, ambitious merchants and all-powerful deities who appear when summoned by the ultimate sacrifices.'

—Kanishk Tharoor, *The Washington Post*

'[The book] reminds us of "human propensities whose lasting power we may prefer to ignore". Imagine *One Thousand and One Nights,* as told not by a young woman but by a Vetāla, a demon whose "whisper is like the crackling sound of a burning house".'

—Alida Becker, *The New York Times Book Review*

'Penick offers an elegant retelling of the *Vetala Panchavimshati*, or 25 tales of betrayal, an eerie 11th-century Sanskrit collection … The highlight is the memorable corpse-spirit, which materializes at will like a nightmare to bedevil the king. This is worth seeking out.'

—*Publishers Weekly*

'Penick deftly handles *[Vikram and Vetāla]* with a translator's eye and a writer's hand. In doing so, he succeeds in conveying the multiplicities of tone: an earthy, at times brutal matter-of-factness, an elegant sensuality which understands the entwining of violence and the body, and touches of humour.'

—Tomoé Hill, *Asymptote Journal*

'[This book] makes the case that stories do not just distil life, but actually enable us to live—especially beyond the physical and temporal limitations of biological life.'

—Oscar Mardell, *The Exacting Clam*

'Penick ... bestows the proper opulence these stories demand; glistening like rubies when delving into the details of vast fortunes or ancient cities, but also like viscera when the tales take a turn for the tragic or macabre.'

—Adam Camiolo, *The Heavy Feather Review*

'Transporting and a joy to read as well as a reflection on the ambiguous power of storytelling to liberate or fetter.'

—Tess Lewis, *Art Fuse*

'Penick's fleet and lyrical retelling draws us back irresistibly into the shimmering abyss of our collective pre-history.'

—Daniil Leiderman, assistant professor, Department of Slavic Languages and Literatures, University of Pittsburgh

'In these twenty-five magnificent tales from an almost unremembered time, our normal human passions appear magnified before us in splendid horror. Each is a tangly vine, ensnaring and twisting the lives of ordinary people, warriors, yogis, princesses, and kings into shapes appalling and unforeseen. You might love it!'

—Late Kidder Smith, former director of Asian Studies, Bowdoin College

'With his mesmerizing recreation of these stories of the Vetāla, Douglas Penick takes part in one of South Asian literature's most enduring practices: to tell stories again and again, in different languages, from differing cultural and religious perspectives. With its lyrical prose, his haunting rendition of the stories offers contemporary readers a version both personal and universal in its appeal.'

—Phyllis Granoff, Lex Hixon Professor Emeritus of Religious Studies, Yale University

'Douglas Penick's retelling of this ancient story cycle is brilliant and irresistible. We are given the mythic backstory of the whole, and it breathes new depth into the tale of King and Corpse. The book's end provides fresh insight into the meaning of the whole. The writing is breathtaking. Words leap off the page rendering the written world as alive as a story told. Profound meanings surface with wild humor and emotion. Beware! You will find yourself in direct confrontation with your own mind as your heart breaks open.'

—Laura Simms, author of *Our Secret Territory: The Secret of Storytelling*

Vikram and Vetāla

A Transformative Retelling

Douglas J. Penick

With an Introduction by

Namita Gokhale

HarperCollins *Publishers* India

First published in the US as a New York Review Books Classic by
New York Review of Books 2024

First published in India by HarperCollins *Publishers* 2026
HarperCollins *Publishers* India, Cyber City,
Building 10-A, Gurugram, Haryana – 122002, India
www.harpercollins.co.in

2 4 6 8 10 9 7 5 3 1

P-ISBN: 978-93-6569-723-0
E-ISBN: 978-93-6569-232-7

Typeset in 11.5/16 Adobe Caslon Pro
by HarperCollins *Publishers* India Pvt. Ltd

Printed and bound at
Nutech Print Services Pvt. Ltd.

FSC
www.fsc.org
MIX
Paper | Supporting responsible forestry
FSC® C195953

This book is printed on FSC® certified paper
which ensures responsible forest management.

*

HarperCollins *Publishers*, Macken House, 39/40 Mayor Street Upper,
Dublin 1, D01 C9W8, Ireland

Contents

Introduction

Namita Gokhale

The Hindu belief system accommodates and honours the spirit world. I began writing this introduction on 19 October 2025. It was an appropriate date, as it was Narak Chaturdashi, Vikram Samvat 2082—a time when ghosts and ghouls emerge before the moonless Amavasya night of Deepawali, the Festival of Lights.

Vikram and Vetāla: A Transformative Retelling is a fascinating rendition of the ancient story cycle of the *Baitâl Pachchisi*. It has travelled across timescapes and culturescapes to be resurrected and given voice by American writer Douglas J. Penick.

These stories address the subtle nuances of both ethical and practical dilemmas through complex questions posed by a vampire-succubus to the exemplary and morally upright King Vikramāditya. They remain part of popular literature, cinema and folk wisdom in contemporary India.

Like many Indians, I encountered the popular Vikram–Vetāla story cycle through television and comic-book representations. It was only much later that I read Chandra Rajan's erudite version and Deepa Agarwal's captivating recountal. The twenty-five tales of the *Baitâl Pachchisi* have inscrutably ancient antecedents.

This gripping story cycle dates back to millennia ago. Its exact antecedents are lost to scholars and literary historians, but we do know of an ancient Indian epic known as the *Brhatkatha*. The literal translation of *Brhatkatha* is 'the Great Narrative'. It is attributed to Gunadhya, a poet who possibly lived in the reign of a Satavana king of Pratishthan (modern-day Paithan in Maharashtra.) Estimated timelines place it between the first century BCE and third century CE. Gunadhya wrote not in Sanskrit but in the now-lost tongue of Paiśaći (literally, language of the demons). Even though the original text of the *Brhatkatha* no longer exists, he is considered on par with the other two inspirational founts of Indian literature, the sages Vyasa and Valmiki.

The loss of a major literary text is always tragic, but stories are not so easily obliterated and have a way of carrying on. The tales from the Brhatkatha were handed down through the centuries and retold in Sanskrit by Kshemendra in the *Brhatkathamanjari* and *Brhatkathaslokasamgraha,* and by Somadeva in the *Kathasaritsagara.*

The fame of the stories spread far and wide. Many of them travelled, over land and by sea, to Western Asia, where they became part of the *One Thousand and One Nights.* Translations into various Indian languages were undertaken by scholars and commissioned by kings and grandees whose interest was piqued by the unusual nature of the moral tales. The Moghuls facilitated Urdu translations. English versions followed as well.

As these tales spread and scattered across the seven seas, they decided to seek further life and interpretation from a mysterious and multifaceted scholar known as Douglas J. Penick. He relied on the *Baitâl Pachchisi—Or The Twenty-Five Tales of a Sprite Translated from the Hindi Text of Dr Duncan Forbes.*

Penick is an unusual and extraordinary scholar with a hunger for forgotten narratives. After undertaking major translations of epic texts from several countries, he has turned his attention to the immortal spectral stories that are so much a part of the popular subculture of Indian thought.

Penick writes, composes and dreams across languages and cultures. He has written texts for opera that have been performed widely. He has penned novels on the third Ming emperor (*Journey of the North Star*) and three book-length episodes from the *Gesar of Ling* epic.

In Boulder, Colorado, in the shadow of the Rocky Mountains, this intrepid storyteller was, in his own words, 'ensnared' by the Vetāla. He declares:

> … a story is something that takes possession of whoever reads or hears it. And it is the Vetāla itself that embodies this demonic aspect of narrative. The life force of a Vetāla, or corpse-demon, derives from the stories it knows and can tell. It may take possession of a corpse for sexual or other kinds of pleasure, but its true power lies in engulfing listeners and readers in the concerns of worlds not their own. […]
>
> Stories, even as they live enduringly within us, never quite integrate themselves into our being. Like a virus, like a symbiont, they condition our existence but are independent of it. Our inner lives are made up of innumerable webs of stories, histories, memories and narratives. At the same time, as we move through life, we are inside other stories, other people's stories, alien histories, floating in an endless sea of tales, fables, gossip. These carry their own domains and linkages within them and they last much longer than we do.

The overarching story of *Vikram and Vetāla* begins with primordial space, beyond time or stasis, void or phenomena. Śiva whispers to the mother of the universe, Pārvatī, telling of fragments of worlds that will come to be.

In another all-too-human world, the son of an oil merchant dreams of Śiva and Pārvatī lying entwined at the mountain summit of a strangely fluid world. Śiva is whispering one story, then another, to Pārvatī; he recounts twenty-five stories in all. In the morning, the man caresses his wife and tells her the stories he had overheard.

He is punished grievously for this unforgivable intrusion, this transgression. Śiva's anger draws out the man's life force and metamorphoses him into a corpse-spirit, a Vetāla. Inside his lifeless body are compressed the twenty-five stories he overheard, which have cost him his life. The corpse is consigned to the branch of a tall tree in a cremation ground, condemned to hang in limbo forever.

The man weeps and pleads for mercy. Śiva takes pity on him and gives him a tenuous escape clause: 'Only if a king will carry you on his back, only if you tell this king all twenty-five stories, only if you can get the king to respond to each story as if it were real, only if, finally, words fail him, only then will you be freed.'

The Vetāla weeps inconsolably. His sense of self is already collapsing into the stories that had possessed him.

I see here a metaphor for the fate of all storytellers who are possessed by their stories. They have to rid themselves of these tales, to pass on the virus, to ensnare another listener.

I shall not rob the stories that follow of their compulsive cliff-hanging suspense. Let readers discover or rediscover the convoluted twists and turns.

I shall, however, discuss the bare outlines of the plot and structure and share some thoughts and observations on how they unfold.

The Indic mind has a propensity for ambiguity. There are no simple answers to the Vetāla's questions. It has been said that Dharma and the path of righteous are hidden in a cave. King Vikramāditya was the very emblem of righteousness. Trapped by the Vetāla, he applied his mind scrupulously to the tricky situations in the stories he was presented with.

The society within which Gunadhyaya originally situated his stories was clearly an intellectually sophisticated one, where thought was applied to moral and ethical issues, as also to equity and legality.

King Vikramāditya's thoughtful resolutions to the conundrums the Vetāla poses show the moral compass of the tales. Let us, for example, examine the resolution to Story 11, 'Love and Ruling'.

> The story was over. The forest was silent. 'O Great King,' asked the corpse-spirit, 'why did the minister die?'
>
> It took King Vikramāditya only a moment to answer.
>
> 'The minister saw that the king would never rule his kingdom, nor would he take responsibility for his people. Eventually, his sensual obsessions would deplete the country.

> The minister knew that to obey the king would lead to the end of his dynasty. He found this unendurable, and he died.'

However, the mind-bending riddles and their solutions are sometimes, to my mind, whimsical or frivolous. This could well be because their contexts, references and allusions have not survived changing societal norms and multiple layers of cultural translation and interpretation.

The narrative structure is an early example of the classic literary device of frame stories. A frame story has a scaffolding that contains another story or set of stories within it. The outer frame, which holds the stories within stories, binds the situations and characters and provides contextuality and cohesion. Scheherazade and the *One Thousand and One Nights* is a well-known example of stories held together by central characters. It is probable that the framing of the *One Hundred and One Nights* was inspired by the *Kathasaritasagara* and *Brhatkatha* formats, as were many of the stories within it.

☠

The literary eloquence of the Vikram–Vetāla stories displays a strong poetic and philosophic imagination. Satire, irony and humour are also masterfully employed. Every shade of mortal and supranatural activity unfolds convincingly before our eyes. Romance, lust, familial love, misfortune, disease and death all play out in these compelling tales.

The tantric sorcerer Ksāntiśīla, the dissembling yogi to whom King Vikramāditya makes his rash commitment, is a caveat against greed and power, politics, religion and superstition. His gruesome end gives a glimpse into the dissolution of evil through the steadfast pursuit of virtue and righteousness.

As we near the resolution of these complex and compelling tales, the Vetāla unburdens himself to King Vikramāditya.

> O Great King Vikramāditya, the twenty-five tales I told have long been the essence of my being. Now they live in you; they are part of your life, and you will carry me into millions of places and times. My existence is inseparable from the story of your life and will continue in whoever hears your history. I will be woven into them. As one tells another, in hundreds of millions of minds, I will become part of hundreds of millions of beings. In aeon after aeon, I will come to life and circumstances beyond imagining and without limit. But now, O Merciful One, my continuing depends upon your survival. Your story must not end. You will have to destroy my long-dead body. Throw it in the fire. It is irrelevant.

To return to Penick's introduction:

> It is through stories and tales and accounts of all kinds that we move continuously, constantly, in and beyond the limits of a single lifespan. Thus we experience what the Śvetāśvatara Upanishad says:
>
> 'You are a woman, and you are a man.
> You are a young man and a maiden,
> And an old one tottering with a staff.
> You are born again facing a new direction.'

And so the stories are born anew and continue through the waves of existence.

Originally published by the *New York Review of Books*, New York, *Vikram and Vetāla: A Transformative Retelling* is a classic rendition of one of the world's eclipsed classics. It returns home with this multilayered retelling as it addresses the riddles of life and death and the worlds beyond.

Prologue

Douglas J. Penick

Throughout my childhood, my mother read stories to me, my brother and my sisters before we went to bed. She read the Bible—both Old and New Testaments—Greek myths, Grimm's Fairy Tales and Andrew Lang's books, among many others. But it was Hans Christian Anderson's *The Little Mermaid* that struck me most deeply and remains in me to this day as a kind of unhealed wound.

More than seventy years after my mother read this story aloud, scenes are still vivid, exactly as I imagined when I first heard them: the bright innocence of glittering green waves breaking on a summer shore; the dream image of someone to be loved, vague and far off; a witch, old and knowing, the embodiment of ancient and implacable transactions; the shadowy claustrophobia of her cave beneath the sea and the growing awareness of an exchange that will be required there; the process of enacting the exchange; pain and the willingness to endure pain; the extraction of the tongue; the willing loss of speech; the awkward loss of familiar limbs and forming of new ones; then moving on an alien land, and the heart-void when longed-for love is a mirage and what remains is unalterable isolation. All these come back as if I had experienced them myself, and recently.

But I have never actually read the story; I may even have stayed away from it., even though it evoked a very specific set of things I seemed to have been born knowing. The story remains a vessel for what has not and perhaps cannot be assimilated but is still present within me. When my mother read it aloud, I was inconsolable. I was six and I wept and wept. I felt this was a subterranean truth, not just in me but perhaps in everyone. My mother's legacy to me was not completely without difficulties, but for this, I am forever deeply beholden to her.

The attraction to the kinds of stories I heard as a child remained. They are, it seems, archaeological fragments found at random, but holding an aspect or aspects of ourselves encased in an unfamiliar language, custom, culture, time and place. Their compression, their assurance and their somewhat inexplicable completeness still exert an enduring seduction as they preserve within us fragments of experience we cannot exactly explain or rationalize or domesticate.

It's not so surprising then that recently, when I had nothing pressing, my love for the *One Thousand and One Arabian Nights* percolated and became the desire to write (or rewrite) that prodigal kind of collection. I searched for something in the public domain and came upon these twenty-five Vetāla tales in an appropriately raw version. They ensnared me. I began writing them down, one after another, even before I'd read them all. I then went over them many times, sometimes expanding, sometimes contracting them. It was a bit like how I imagine painting a mural, moving from large underpainted volumes to ever-smaller details. I enjoyed the process a great deal. I found that while the plots rarely provided the sense of order we find in more familiar stories, moments within these tales became strangely meaningful. Not in the way that wise sayings or surprising insights are meaningful, but in the way that clouds will suddenly seem, for a moment, to be expressing some kind of wordless but intensely vivid significance.

The Baitâl Pachchisi, retold here as *Vikram and Vetāla*, is said to be one of the oldest story collections in existence. It was written down more than a thousand years ago, but the stories themselves are all at least two or three times as old. This famous and feared collection lives in many ancient as well as modern languages. It embodies the continuity of human propensities whose lasting power we may often prefer to ignore. Here, it is retold in English with the same stories in the same order as in the ancient Hindi *Baitâl Pachchisi* (see Notes). The questions and answers, which are an integral part of that collection, are also reproduced here in the same way as in the original.

In the story that frames the Vetāla tales, there is a famously able king, Vikramāditya, who is tricked into playing a part in the schemes of a power-mad yogi, and he is conned over and over into continuing this role. There is the Vetāla, a corpse who lives when retelling the stories that continue to entrap the king. The king is caught in illusions produced by a corpse; his life is imprisoned in tales from the past, tales of deception from times that are no more. And all of this is at the behest of the yogi, as he seeks to control the world and to rewrite history.

In these stories, characters' identities do not derive from their inner lives. As is generally typical in earlier kinds of narrative, there is limited concern with psychology beyond social caste and such arbitrary designations as young, old, beautiful, ugly, brave, cowardly, generous, wise, foolish, proud, rich, poor, etc. More complex inner aspects of identity, personal development or the continuity of individual consciousness as it unfolds in the context of socio-historical phenomena—these things are of little concern, if they are considered to exist at all.

What we see here are people possessed by deities, social roles and passions; they are captured and moved by lust, hate, covetousness, desire for place and power. These are the harsh intensities that fly invisibly through the air until they seize and, with violent caprice, take control of unsuspecting people, regardless of caste, gender, age. This a world of continuous, indiscriminate, impersonal cruelty. The most common of these passions, at least in the Vetāla tales, is love. Falling in love, whether mutual or one-sided, is something that arrives from outside as lovers are struck by the arrows of lust shot from Kama, the God of Desire's, bow. It's unaccountable, haphazard, all-consuming and it defines the lover's fate ever after. Envy, hatred, spiritual ambition and a desire for wealth or power proceed similarly as men and women fall prey to these exacting masters. Plots or stories all begin and are shaped by these interventions, which dictate the possibilities and outcomes available to an otherwise unsuspecting person.

Similarly, a story is something that takes possession of whoever reads or hears it. And it is the Vetāla itself that embodies this demonic aspect of narrative. The life-force of a Vetāla, or corpse-demon, derives from the stories it knows and can tell. It may take possession of a corpse for sexual or other kinds of pleasure, but its true power lies in engulfing listeners and readers in the concerns of worlds not their own. In these stories, the Vetāla keeps the king under its power by requiring him to judge elements of the story as if they were 'real'. The king's answers do not reconcile but expose the irreconcilable gap between the world of passions, enchantments and transformations and the domains of laws, reasons and judgement. Likewise, we, the readers, may hope that the stories we hear and the world we live in exist harmoniously, that one may inform and enrich the other, but in the end, there is no real requirement that this be so. Stories, even as they live enduringly within us, never quite integrate themselves into our being. Like a virus, like a symbiont, they condition our existence but are independent of it. Our inner lives are made up of innumerable webs of stories, histories, memories and narratives. At the same time, as we move through life, we are inside other stories, other people's stories, alien histories, floating in an endless sea of tales, fables, gossip. These carry their own domains and linkages within them and they last much longer than we do. Our existence beyond the bounds of a single life, as well as our posterity, depends entirely on them, on becoming one of them. It is through stories and tales and accounts of all kinds that we move continuously, constantly, in and beyond the limits of a single lifespan. Thus, we experience what the Śvetāśvatara Upanishad says:

> 'You are a woman, and you are a man.
> You are a young man and a maiden,
> And an old one tottering with a staff.
> You are born again facing in a new direction.
> You are the blue fly and the red-eyed parrot,
> The cloud pregnant with lightning, with thunder,
> You are the seasons and the seas,
> The beginningless, the abiding
> From whom the spheres are born.'[1]

---

1 Śvetāśvatara Upanishad 4.1–4 from Śaiva u; Kalyāna, Upanisad anka (Gorakhpur: Gita Press, 1949).

Before Beginning I

As has been told:

Primordial space, the undivided, the signless, where sentience and non-sentience, awareness and unawareness, have not divided, where there is neither life nor death, nor time nor stasis, continuity or discontinuity, void or phenomena. Primordial Sea undivided, Primordial Sky undivided, Primordial Darkness undivided, Primordial Light undivided. Chaos moving and alive without reference to order or disorder. Neither noun nor verb. Continuity continuing in its own reference. A vast and empty luminous expanse.

Sounds, words emerge, undivided from the original sea, never separated nor born. Phenomena rippling on the surface of the sea. Rippling as great forces, gods, cycles of time wherein worlds and universes are born, evolve, decay, die, and dissolve. Whispers pass by, not remembered, nor forgotten.

Before Beginning II

As has been told:

Amongst whispered ripples of the Primordial Sea, ripples flowing one into another, chasing, following, continuing, the whisperings ebbing, from this momentary surface. These continuing now and now and now, merging and dissolving and re-emerging as form, as Śiva, as Śiva, enfolding, whispering to Pārvatī, as Pārvatī listening, enfolded. Mount Kailash rising, wave-crest moving slowly, at the highest point, the border of solidity, where, amid ceaseless winds, it touches an ever-changing sky. Śiva whispers to the mother of the universe, to Pārvatī, whispers idly, and his whisperings tell fragments of worlds that will come to be, that will seem. Extending long pale arms, Śiva reaches down into the chaos of the lightless sea, draws up his hands and shimmering droplets fall, whispering of moments, stories unconstrained by meanings, shaped from chaos by falling, whispering, caressing as they circle in the whorls of Pārvatī's inner ear. She sighs, exhales in deeper languor, smiles slightly. They are entwined; they merge and emerge; as he speaks, elements of a broken history of the world appear.

A Wave Beginning

And so, as it was told:

Long, long ago, near Vārānasī, in a white house on the shore of the great Ganges, lived a man named Brahman, the son of an oil merchant. He had inherited his father's trade and was married but had no children. One summer night, as the green waters of the river flowed to the sea, Brahman slept next to his wife and dreamed. The flickering waters echoed in his mind. He dreamed he saw Śiva and Pārvāti lying entwined at the mountain summit of a strangely fluid world. He gazed in awe at their vast coupling. He could not help hearing Śiva's low rumbling as he delighted Pārvatī, whispering one story, then another, twenty-five in an unbroken stream.

In the morning, when he woke, Brahman could not help himself. He made love to his wife and told her these stories as he had heard them.

Śiva heard the echo of his words and stories vibrating in the air below. Someone in another time and place was retelling, repeating moments from his desire. But tales that had sparkled on the lips of gods, when translated into lower realms, became hard and broken things. Such crude, constricted distortions aggravated the great Śiva's vast and subtle being. That faint magic remained pained him more. Before this moment, stories did not exist in the world of men and women. But now and forever, people would invent tales without end. True or false, once something was said, others would repeat it, even if they didn't believe it. And there would be no end to the number of repetitions and transformations that stirred people's minds. Men and women would soon be completely unable to distinguish the human realm from stories about the human realm. The Great God was enraged that the intimacy of his love—the merging, caressing passions, the scents and colours and textures emerging and dissolving as he moved within the Great Goddess, whispering and licking—that this play of love should somehow be overheard, that its expressions be somehow stolen and used to debase a world and corrupt it by names and forms. Thus opened the floodgates of some deeper, more indifferent and terrifying fate.

Without a thought, Śiva saw this oil-seller's son, this Brahman, lying with his wife in a white house beside the languid Ganges. He pulled the man's consciousness from his body. The body fell lifeless. The wife screamed. Śiva held the man's life force, minute, shimmering, wriggling as it sought new embodiment. He sealed it back inside the corpse, sprinkling it with droplets, each carrying a story the man had once heard. The corpse, filled with seething mist, now was neither alive nor dead.

Śiva hung the corpse by the feet from a tall Śinśipa tree in a boundaryless charnel ground. The corpse-spirit was confined inside the desiccated man-shaped sack, now filled with the echoes of those tales he had so unfortunately heard and so unwisely told. He howled. He begged for Śiva to let him go. He screamed. It would be better to be destroyed completely. He had not meant to trespass in the private world of gods. It was an accident. Śiva, in his way, took pity on the fool: 'Stupid man, the stories you stole are now the reason you exist. Only if a king will carry you on his back, only if you tell this king all twenty-five stories, only if you can get this king to respond to each story as if it were real, only if finally, words fail him, only then will you be freed.'

Brahman—though already his sense of himself as the bearer of this name was fading—heard this curse and wept. He was increasingly unable to separate the stories he had so disastrously heard and told from any other mode of being.

A Tide of Tales: King Vikramāditya

And this tale began:

In a time now at the edge of memory, in west central India, stood the black-walled city of Dhar, 'The City of Swords'. The king of Dhar, Gandharvasena, had six sons, all of whom were intelligent and vigorous. When Gandharvasena died, his eldest son became king, but his younger son, Vikramāditya, had no doubt that destiny had chosen him to rule. He killed his elder brother and took the throne. Vikramāditya was brilliant, courageous, just, generous and indomitable. His skills as a natural ruler soon made him famous. He ruled from his Golden Lion Throne and extended his domain across the subcontinent. In time, however, he became tired of conquest and the duties of ruling. He renounced his kingdom and set out to explore beyond the borders of the world he knew. He gave his younger brother Bathari the throne. Dressed as a beggar, he walked into the forest and left his kingdom behind.

At that time a Brahmin priest, renowned for travelling to and from celestial realms, ascended to the Great God Krishna's heavenly domain. There he found a coral tree with jade leaves, which bore the golden apples of immortality. He plucked one of these shining honey-scented fruit and, on his return to earth, gave it to his wife. 'Eat this and you will never die,' he told her.

But she burst into tears. 'No, no, no. Take it away,' she wailed. 'This will only bring me unending torment and suffering. O Beloved Husband, you will die, but I will live on. I'll see brothers and sisters, and all my friends die. Worst of all, I will have to watch the deaths of all my children and all their children and their children's children. By then, my wealth will be exhausted, my servants will have run off or died, my house will be a ruin, my farms will fall fallow. I will be ancient, feeble, blind and deaf, destitute, homeless and alone. Death, O Wise Husband, is better,' she said.

The Brahmin knew she was right. 'Give it to the king,' she begged. 'Surely he will reward you with gold and jewels. We can use them while we are both alive.'

The Brahmin did as she advised.

King Bathari was delighted with the Brahmin's golden apple and rewarded him with three sacks of gems and fifty bars of gold. The king then gave this marvellous apple to his beautiful wife. He loved her more deeply than life itself; he did not know about her faithlessness, her predatory lust. This treacherous queen gave the fruit to the king's most trusted bodyguard, the tallest and most handsome officer of all his soldiers, who had for a long time been her secret lover. This officer himself was insatiably lecherous; he gave the fruit to a slender, conniving courtesan who was his latest mistress. This clever woman decided to gain the king's favour by giving him the magical fruit. She hoped he might even make her queen. King Bathari accepted the gift and rewarded the courtesan with great wealth, but he guessed what had happened and was sick at heart.

'What did you do with the celestial fruit I gave you?' he asked his queen.

'I ate it,' she replied.

King Bathari now understood his wife's utter faithlessness and the disloyalty of those he had believed in. He saw clearly that worldly happiness was an illusion, all relationships impermanent and all ambitions futile. In despair, he, like his brother before, abandoned the Gold Lion Throne of Dhar and, in beggar's rags, left his capital.

With the throne empty, there was no one to maintain order, to protect the people, to support the sages and make offerings to the gods. The kingdom fell into chaos. Lawlessness and violence attracted a rapacious demon who took possession of the royal palace. The demon's black body swelled like a thundercloud, blocking the sun and filling the air with poisonous green smoke. He had wild orange hair and a tiny red mouth. He devoured whoever resisted him. He ruled by confusion and terror.

When Vikramāditya heard of this, he returned to take back his throne. The demon met Vikramāditya outside the great bronze gates of Dhar and refused to surrender. For two nights and one day the two fought violently. The people looked down from the walls in awe and fear. Finally, as the sun came up a second time, Vikramāditya used the last of his strength to hurl the demon to the ground. He stood on the demon's neck and began to choke the life out of him.

'Great King,' the demon croaked, 'I am defeated. Let me up. I swear I can give you something that will allow you to avoid the suffering you are fated to endure.'

'Monster!' shouted Vikramāditya. 'I can kill you in a second. How can you spare me from anything?'

'Sire, if you listen to what I have to tell, I promise you will escape a life of endless confusion and terrible pain. My story holds the secret of your past and the key to your future. If you take what I tell you to heart, you will have a long and happy life. Your reign will never be forgotten. The world will recount your deeds forever.'

'And you swear you will leave this place and never return?'

'I swear.'

'And never again will you trouble me or my people?'

'I promise.'

'You agree that you are forever bound by these promises?'

'I am bound, sire.'

Vikramāditya freed the demon. The two then sat side by side in front of the bronze gates, and the king listened to the demon's tale.

The Demon's Story

Many years ago, O Great Warrior, when your father, Gandharvasena, was at the start of his illustrious rule, he was wandering in the forest alone. On the outskirts of a cremation ground, he encountered a shocking sight: an ascetic, a small dark man wearing only a blue loincloth, was hanging head down, tied by a rope around his ankles to the highest branch of a Nimba tree. This yogi, whose name was Valkalāśana, the Bark-Eater, was wreathed in smoke from a bonfire below him. He had no food or water. He lived by inhaling smoke, eating bark and drinking sap. He did not respond when the king spoke to him, and when the king prodded him with a stick, he did not react. The king saw that the yogi was in a state of utter detachment and knew that such ascetics could have enormous worldly powers. They were able, it was said, to secure the success and good fortune of those they blessed. Even so, King Gandharvasena was incensed that someone living in his kingdom could be so indifferent to him. The thought enraged him.

Quickly the king returned to his palace throne room and summoned his court. He described what he had seen and offered enough gold to support a large family for ten generations to whoever brought the yogi to serve him at court. A pale young courtesan with strange blue eyes stood up.

'O King, if you allow me, I will bring him here.'

'You? But how?'

'I will have a child by this man, and he will carry the child to court on his shoulder.'

'You swear you can do this?'

'Sire, to earn the great fortune you have promised, I swear I will do it. In a year's time, you will see.'

The clever courtesan made her way through the forest and found the yogi hanging upside down from the branches of a Nimba tree. She hid in the woods and watched him for days. It was just as the king had said. The man was ash brown and shrivelled like a catalpa pod. The fire below him never dwindled, and he lived on smoke, small amounts of bark and tree sap.

The courtesan smiled. She had come prepared. She moved close to the yogi and put a tiny piece of sugar between his parched lips. At first, he didn't move; then slowly he sucked on the candy. He gave a little smile. Over the next few days, he ate more and more sugar. His appetite returned; he opened his eyes and gazed at her. She fed him water, then milk, then rice, until the rope no longer held him and he crashed to the ground. The smoking fire vanished. Then all the appetites of a normal man returned. The yogi was overcome with lust. He slept with the courtesan and she became pregnant.

In nine months, she gave birth to a boy. The child looked at his father expectantly, but the yogi was filled with revulsion and bitterness. What had he done? Again, he had been trapped in the realms of sensuous illusion and worldly obligations. What could he do?

The courtesan understood all this very well. She said to the fallen ascetic: 'Ah, Swami, we must go to the capital. Carry your son on your shoulders. You and I will confess what we have done. The king will know what you should do.'

When the man with his child and the beautiful, blue-eyed woman stood before King Gandharvasena, he remembered her and the promises they had exchanged. He gave her the gold as promised. The yogi suddenly realized that the king had debased him to demonstrate the superiority of worldly power. Mad with rage, he pulled the infant from his shoulder and, holding it by its feet, swung it violently round and round over his head. The baby screamed and suddenly its body ripped apart. Its head landed at the king's feet. Its torso flew into the house of a nearby potter. Its bloody legs and feet slipped from the yogi's grip, flew through the air and landed on the roof of an oil merchant's house.

The king and his courtiers were stunned in horror. The yogi disappeared in a clap of thunder. No one spoke of this ever again.

The demon fell silent and gazed at King Vikramāditya. Wisps of green smoke leaked from around his bloodshot eyes. The king waited to hear the point of this tale.

'Now, Great King,' the demon's whisper was like the crackling sound of a burning house, 'like all stories, this reveals a pattern hidden in your life. Perhaps you now will see how to escape your fate. Pay attention. Ten months after this terrible event, in each household where parts of the unfortunate child's body had landed, a wife gave birth to a boy. These three boys were born not just on the same day but at the same hour, the same minute, the same second. The same planets, stars and constellations marked their births. They were bound together by fate more closely than brothers.

'You, sire, of the three boys, are obviously the son born to a king. Soon you will meet the others. The boy born to a potter will seek to shape earth's common clay according to his will. The boy born into an oil-seller's house will learn what it means to be like the husk of a sesame seed whose oil has been pressed out. Each of you has a life that emerged from a single story long ago. Your lives will be woven together again in another tale. You cannot escape this. But if you see the pattern, you may find a way to change the outcome. Thus, O Protector of the World, I have given you the key to your fate.'

With that, the demon vanished like a hurricane, dissolving into a pale blue sky.

☠

And so Vikramāditya again assumed the Golden Lion Throne of Dhar. He led his armies to victory and brought prosperity to his kingdom. He built palaces, temples, universities and parks; his capital became a beacon of culture. He held court, resolved disputes and received innumerable offerings from those seeking his favour. The demon's tale faded from his memory.

One day, during the twentieth year of his reign, an ascetic named Ksāntiśīla, very dark, bony, with wild hair, bloodshot eyes, black teeth, long yellow fingernails and wearing bone ornaments, came before King Vikramāditya. He gave a deep bow, slowly extended his hands and offered the king a large red mango, perfect and luscious. The king's steward accepted the offering and put it on a silver plate. The king thanked the yogi, who bowed again, sat and waited. After a few hours, he went away. King Vikramāditya watched the yogi leave. Something bothered him, but he brushed it aside. His steward put the mango in a cabinet with other gifts.

For the next twenty-five days, the yogi Ksāntiśīla would return and give King Vikramāditya a perfect mango. The king's steward would accept the gifts and put them in the cabinet. On the twenty-fifth day, the steward became distracted. He accidentally dropped the fruit and it split apart. From its centre, a large ruby the colour of pigeon's blood rolled out onto the white marble floor. An attendant brought it to the king. King Vikramāditya loved jewels; his coffers were filled with diamonds, sapphires, emeralds and rubies, and he could never have enough. And this ruby, the size of a hen's egg, was by far the finest, most beautiful jewel he had ever seen. He could not imagine its value or how the yogi had obtained it.

'Why have you given me such an extraordinary thing?' King Vikramāditya asked the yogi the next time he appeared.

'Sire,' Ksāntiśīla replied, 'even a lowly mendicant such as I knows that when one visits kings, spiritual teachers, astrologers, physicians or beautiful women, one should present gifts that properly honour them. Such beings have the power to provide one with benefits far more valuable than any offering.'

'And for this ruby?' the king asked.

'O Sire, why do you speak of a single jewel when there is its equal in each mango I've given you?'

The king called for the other mangoes to be cut open. Indeed, inside each was an identical ruby of extraordinary beauty, lustre and value. Heaped on a tray, they glowed like embers.

The jewels dazzled King Vikramāditya. He was overwhelmed with delight but then wondered if he had been trapped.

'O Holy Yogi, you must know that no jewels in the world equal these. They are more valuable than all my possessions together. And, as you have observed, such a gift is given in anticipation of receiving something greater. So, even if I accepted your offerings without knowing their worth, now I must repay you in some extraordinary way. Tradition and law require me to do this. Tell me what you desire.'

The yogi pressed his palms together and gave a thin smile. 'O King, my request must be a secret. Just as with magic spells, mantras, medical formulas, vows and spiritual practices, family affairs and secret vices, this should not be spoken in public. Whatever is heard by three pairs of ears is no longer secret, but even Brahma himself will never know what one man has heard.'

The king nodded and led the yogi to a small courtyard garden with a splashing fountain, which masked whatever anyone there might say. He concealed his apprehensions and asked: 'You have put me in your debt. Tell me now what you want.'

'Sire, I am a humble yogi who has endured great suffering and practised austerities all my adult life. I have learned the pain and futility of worldly desires. I have renounced earthly concerns and cultivated the spiritual life. Now I am on the verge of achieving a kind of wisdom no mortal man has even glimpsed. Soon, on a night dictated by the position of the stars, I will go to a charnel ground on the banks of the Godavari River. There I will set out offerings and chant secret invocations. If you, my king, do what I require, I will, without doubt, accomplish something so great that all mankind will bow down and all gods will reward. You, sire, will be forever renowned for bringing my endeavours to fruition.'

King Vikramāditya was suddenly alert; this must be the incarnation of the potter's son of whom the demon once spoke. Whatever pattern was to be completed now could not be escaped. It was his fate. 'As you know, I must grant your request. Just tell me what you wish.'

The yogi smiled and nodded. 'Promise me that you will come, alone and armed, on Tuesday after sunset in the month of Bhadon, when the moon is dark and monsoon rains keep everyone indoors. I will be waiting for you at the cremation ground beside the River Godāvari. There is a task you must perform for me. I will tell you then.'

'I give you my word: I will do as you request,' the king vowed.

Three months later, Ksāntiśīla sent a message to King Vikramāditya. Now was the time for him to fulfil his pledge. To rouse his resolve, the king made offerings to Mahādevī, the Great Goddess. Then, dressed in dark clothes and chain mail and armed with his long sword, he stepped out into the roaring winds and rain of the monsoon. The king was soaked as he made his way to the charnel ground, where he found Ksāntiśīla, looking like a hell-demon, sitting amid flickering cremation fires. Beneath a small tent, he was praying before a mandala he had drawn on the ground; he had an imposing array of offerings ready to present. Lightning flashed and thunder roared as the winds screamed high in the trees. The air was filled with wrathful spirits and ghosts, swirling in the smoke. Vikramāditya was sure he saw the shadows of women dancing and heard the voices of children chanting. The yogi joined the singing and struck two skulls together in rhythm to the unearthly songs.

'What do you wish me to do?' King Vikramāditya asked grimly. The yogi continued beating the skulls; he looked coldly at the king. 'Four miles to the southwest is an abandoned cemetery and at its centre is a Śinśipā tree. Hanging from the highest branch is a Vetāla, an ancient corpse with a living being trapped inside. Cut it down and bring it to me. Then do as I say, and I will be able to complete the rites necessary to attain the powers I seek. This will end your obligation to me. You can leave and enjoy the riches I have given you. But this errand is not so simple as it might seem. You must not speak to the corpse-spirit. If you do, it will vanish and return to the tree where you found it. You will have to begin all over again.' The king, anxious to be done with his task, nodded and strode off.

King Vikramāditya trudged through night and storm. Wind pulled at his hair; hot rain whipped his face and chest. He felt he was struggling among hordes of hungry ghosts and demons. Snakes emerged from beside the path and coiled around his legs. When he reached the abandoned cemetery, the storm suddenly stopped. Clouds of fog rose from the ground all around him in the form of misshapen ghouls, writhing, digging up graves and devouring corpses. The air smelled of blood and rotting meat. On the perimeter of the burial grounds, he could see jackals with glowing green eyes stalking among the trees and howling.

Had Vikramāditya been a king who had lived only in court, he would have collapsed in terror, but years of battles, of wandering in strange lands, had prepared him for the most violent and grotesque encounters.

Then he saw an ancient Śinśipā tree, its leaves and branches pulsing with a blue phosphorescent glow. In the high winds, invisible demons were yowling: 'Kill him.' 'Kill.' 'Kill.' And hanging from the highest branch at the centre of the tree, suspended by a rope, was a corpse, luminous white and smelling of rot. It swayed gently in the air. 'So, this is the corpse-demon, the Vetāla that the yogi wants,' said Vikramāditya to himself. He climbed the tree, unsheathed his sword and cut the rope. The body fell softly to the ground, emitting a high, keening sigh. The king climbed down but before he picked up the body, he asked: 'Do you have a name?'

Immediately, the body flew into the air, the rope again became whole, and the corpse was hanging from the tree. The king quickly climbed the tree and again cut the rope. The Vetāla drifted to the ground; the king followed. 'Who are you, monstrous thing?'

Again, the body floated up and was suspended from the tree. Again, the king followed and cut the thing down. This time he said nothing. He sheathed his sword and swung the corpse-demon over his shoulder. The Vetāla was weightless but strangely dense and felt like a cape of cold mist. The king straightened his shoulders and, carrying his ghostly burden, began his journey back to the charnel ground and the waiting yogi.

As they walked through the misty night, the Vetāla whispered in a high silvery voice: 'Who are you? Where are you taking me?'

The king was determined not to answer, but the effort was painful. 'You may speak,' the spirit hissed.

Vikramāditya then told the demon about the yogi, the rubies, his promise and the task he must now fulfil.

The corpse-spirit sighed. 'Your task will start over whenever you speak to me. And if I ask a question, you must answer. If you try to remain silent, you will experience unimaginable, unendurable pain. So, you must answer, and I will then return to the tree where you found me. Your task will end only when you truly cannot answer what I ask.'

The king could see no escape, nor any way to end this task; he was trapped and would have to carry this ethereal burden through the dark until he could find a way out.

They had not gone far when the corpse-spirit again whispered, 'O Great King, this world we now traverse together is, as you know, a sea of insatiable desires cruel deceits. Let me distract you with stories from other places and times.'

The king nodded. What choice did he have? In its silky whisper, the corpse-spirit began.

STORY 1

True Love

Pratāpamukauta, a king known for his tolerance, ruled from the white-walled city of Vārānasī. His son, Prince Vajramukuta, was brave, open-hearted and exceedingly handsome, but unfortunately, not very intelligent. Fortunately, the prince had a loyal friend, Buddhisena, the prime minister's son, a young man unusually shrewd and wise.

One day, the two went hunting. Joyously, they chased and killed deer, foxes, doves and pheasants until they found themselves tired, their horses worn out, deep in an unfamiliar part of the forest. As they rode on, they entered a well-tended park of unimaginable beauty, an expanse that seemed more celestial than earthly. At the centre of the park's lush green lawn was a large circular pond that resembled a disc of polished silver. Beyond the pool, a temple of white and pink marble shone in the humid air. The park was surrounded by towering palms swaying and shimmering like giant peacock feathers. Snow geese, emerald-headed ducks, blue cranes, white egrets and all kinds of water birds swam in the pool and nested in the trees without fear or care. On the water's surface, lotuses floated, bloomed and swayed in the warm fragrant breeze. This garden, its jewel-like flowers, enchanting birdsong and intoxicating perfumes seemed like a place where the Great

Goddess Mahādevī herself might dwell when she shows herself as the embodiment of passion and love.

The young men dismounted at the pond's edge and washed their faces. They turned to the temple, bowed and began to offer prayers. They had not completed their devotions when a young woman of extraordinary grace and beauty emerged from the temple. She wore a robe of white silk brocade and was radiant as a summer moon; her smile and sparkling glances were those of a goddess. She was surrounded by a retinue of women her age wearing robes in all the colours of the rainbow. The young woman seemed to hover above the ground amid her entourage as they came to the water's edge to bathe. The prince had no doubt that he was looking at a goddess.

For a moment the two found themselves staring deep into each other's eyes. 'Ah, Kama, God of Desire, you have taken possession of my soul,' the prince groaned aloud. Indeed, both were pierced by the God of Love's five arrows, and overcome first with languor, then infatuation, then fever, then craving and finally obsession. As the young woman stepped into the pool, the two continued to gaze at each other from afar. When she emerged from the water, droplets streaming off her robes, and went with her attendants to walk in the shade of the trees, time seemed to stop. The prince thought he was dreaming as he walked towards her. When he came near, the princess looked at him inquisitively, took a lotus flower that she had twined in her hair and held it to her ear. Then she bit the flower, stopped, put it under her right foot, then retrieved it and placed it between her breasts. Finally, the enchantment ended; the princess and her maids-in-waiting returned to waiting carriages, which spirited them away.

As they rode back to his father's palace, Prince Vajramukuta was in despair. 'What can I do, my friend?' he asked Buddhisena. 'I cannot bear it. If I can't find her, my heart will stop. But I don't know her name. I have no idea where she comes from. What can I do?'

The minister's son said nothing. He thought that once home, the prince's passion would fade. But after a week, the prince was still obsessed. He would not eat or drink. He sighed. He could not sleep. He did not come to court when his father asked for him. Then Buddhisena said to the prince: 'My lord, think again. All the world knows that those who wander on the paths of love do not survive. As long as they live, love inflicts a thousand cuts, and with each cut, their life force wanes.'

'Ah,' the prince cried out. 'Whether my fate is pleasure or pain, I will never turn away.'

The minister's son then knew that he had no choice but to help the prince achieve his goal. He asked: 'My Lord, when she left, did this woman say anything to you or you to her?'

'No. Nothing.' The prince sighed.

'But didn't she make certain signs? Do you remember them?'

'Yes, yes, I think I do …' the prince thought back. 'I think she took a lotus blossom from her hair; after that, she put it to her ear, then bit it and placed it under her foot. Then she lifted the lotus and placed it between her breasts.'

'Yes, that's how I remember it too,' said the minister's son.

'But do you think that all that meant something?' asked the prince.

'I do,' replied the minister's son. 'She was telling you her name, the name of her homeland and certain other things too.'

'Really?' The prince could barely control his excitement. 'Tell me.'

'Listen, O Lord. When she moved the lotus from the side of her head down to her ear, she was indicating that she comes from the south, from Karnakubja, the place where Karnatic singing began. By biting the flower, she told you that she is the daughter of King Dantāghatā, which means "bite". Pressing the lotus under her foot, she showed that her name is Padmāvatī, "she who is like a lotus". When she pressed the lotus to her heart, she showed you that you have entered her heart.'

Now the prince was beside himself with excitement. The minister's son and he left for Karnakubja immediately. They rode day and night, and two days later, they were standing in the evening light outside the high red-brick walls of King Dantāghatā's palace. They were awed by its grandeur. Suddenly they were exhausted and urgently needed a place to sleep. Across the square from the palace gate, an old woman was spinning cotton in front of her house. Buddhisena approached her, bowed and began: 'Honoured mother, we are merchants who have just arrived here. Our goods will follow soon, but we need a place to stay.'

The woman saw that the young men were of noble bearing, and she offered them lodging.

Next morning, as they all sat together drinking tea, the old woman chatted on about how the king had given her this house. She had been the wet nurse of his daughter, Princess Padmāvatī, and still the princess wanted her nearby. In fact, she would wait on the princess that very evening.

The prince could not contain himself. 'O Madam, could you be kind enough to tell her that the prince whom she saw by the pool near Vārānasī has come to see her?' And he blurted out the story of his meeting with the princess.

The old woman understood perfectly and relished being a party to romantic intrigue. She smiled. 'Why wait? I'll go to her right now.'

Princess Padmāvatī was sitting alone, watching red finches nesting in the palace gardens, when her old nurse arrived. She bowed her head to receive the old woman's blessing. 'O my child, when you were a baby, I gave you my milk. All I think about is your happiness. Now I must tell you that the prince whose heart you captured by the pool in Vārānasī has come here. He understood the meaning of your gestures. He is a good choice for you. He will make you happy.'

But with that, the princess seemed enraged. She spat on the fingers of both hands and spread the spit on the sole of one of her sandals. Suddenly, she slapped her old nurse on the face with the sandal. The nurse was stunned and hobbled back to her house as quickly as she could.

The old lady wept as she told the two men what had happened, and the prince was overcome with despair. But Buddhisena laughed. 'Your Majesty, do not be downcast. Kind hostess, do not be disturbed. When you understand things properly, you will rejoice.'

'Explain then,' cried the prince.

'Using all ten fingers to wet her sandal, the princess meant that when the ten nights of moonlight have come to an end, she will meet you in the dark. Slapping you, kind lady, meant that she had to reject the prince until then.'

The prince and nurse were delighted.

When the day and time finally came, the nurse returned to the palace to bring the princess to her suitor. She found the princess had put saffron paste on three of her fingers. Suddenly the girl lashed out and again struck her old nurse. She hissed: 'Get out of here!'

The old woman was shocked beyond words. She wept as she returned to her house. She told the two men what had happened, but the minister's son was undisturbed. 'Do not worry. The meaning here is not what you think. The princess is in the state that afflicts all women every month. After three days have passed, go see her again.'

On the fourth day, when the old nurse came to her, the princess, with great coldness, had guards expel her from the Western Gate. The nurse was again distraught. The prince was frustrated and depressed. But his clever companion explained. 'Go now and wait for the princess at that same gate. She is going to let you in.'

At the appointed time, the prince, armed with his sword and camouflaged in dark brown robes, hurried through the sleeping city. He waited anxiously in the shadows. The princess opened the gate and saw him. Their eyes met and they laughed with joy. She pulled him through the gate, closed it behind them and brought him to a bridal chamber decked with white roses and gardenias, furnished with divans covered in silver brocade, perfumed by censers filling the air with musk and attar of roses. Trays of confections were laid out everywhere and with them golden goblets and pitchers of cool wine. Everywhere, the walls were covered with jewel-like paintings of lovers in all the stages of courtship and lovemaking. The princess's attendants, all dressed in translucent silks, smiled and laughed.

The prince was immersed in a world of pleasure and delight. The princess washed his feet. 'I wish only to serve you, Great Lord. You have gone to such lengths to see me. Let me fan you with peacock feathers and give you wine.'

They talked and laughed throughout what was left of the night, and when the sun rose, she concealed him until the next night. Then they devoted themselves to intricate and unceasing amorous pleasures. The following month was lost in bliss, delirium, languor.

But one night, when Princess Padmāvatī had needed to withdraw for a time, Prince Vajramukuta gazed through a high window at the crescent moon. For all that he had been enjoying unimaginable pleasures he believed could exist only in celestial realms, he felt guilty. 'How could I be so selfish?' he thought. 'How could I have forgotten my dearest friend? He has made my happiness possible. What can Buddhisena be thinking of me now?'

When the princess returned to him, she wondered at his altered mood. 'What has disturbed you, my Prince? Have I failed in any way to please you?'

'Ah, Princess, you have opened more doors to delights of the body and transports of heart than I ever imagined. But I have a loyal and wise companion, the son of my father's chief minister. He has been my unfailing friend and advisor all my life. But now, he has not heard a word from me for a month. It is he who interpreted your gestures and brought us together. I have treated him unfairly.'

The princess was silent for a while, then replied, 'Now I understand. Your desire to leave me, if only for an hour, to ease your friend's anxiety, is an expression of the nobility of your character.'

She kissed him and held him tightly. 'Very well, my love. Go at once. You are my joy. Honour your dear friend and console him for your absence. I will send a banquet. Feast together. Return to me when you have eased your misgivings and made your friend content.'

When Prince Vajramukuta had left, the princess was consumed with rage. She whispered orders to her servants to prepare a great array of savoury meat dishes and confections, all suffused with deadly poisons, and to take them to the house where the prince and his friend were staying.

The prince and the minister's son, Buddhisena, were overjoyed to see each other once again. Soon, a parade of servants from the princess's palace appeared and set out a lavish banquet before them. The minister's son asked his happy friend: 'How is it, my lord, that the princess has sent us this wonderful feast?'

The prince then told the whole story of how he missed Buddhisena, how the princess saw his unhappy state and encouraged him to rejoin his friend. She sent this extraordinary feast so that they could celebrate their reunion. The prince was about to offer his friend a dish of fragrant lamb stewed with walnuts when the minister's son abruptly raised his hand. 'Stop, sire! Do not touch this food. Do not even touch the plate.'

The prince was puzzled by his friend's sudden severity. Buddhisena looked at his lord with concern. 'It was not, I regret, so wise to mention our friendship.'

'Can you suspect that someone who has given me such complete proof of her love would wish me harm?'

'Look!' said Buddhisena. The minister's son took the plate of lamb and had it given to a stray dog. The dog tasted the meat, collapsed, writhed violently and died.

'Treacherous demoness! How could I ever have loved her? We should leave here right now.'

But the prince's friend smiled. 'Your Highness, as you have been told, Mahādevī, the Great Goddess, is the body of the world. She is lust itself. And lust is fate. Fate joined you and this princess. She cannot help that her passion will allow nothing to interrupt it. You cannot end your love because she is angry.'

'So now what?' the prince asked.

'Weave this passion, this great love, into your life. The princess must leave her palace here and live with you in Varānāsi. Is this not what truly you desire?'

'If it does not offend you, dear friend, then yes. This is what I want. Tell me how to accomplish it.'

'My Lord, go back to the palace immediately. Take this trident with you. Tell the princess that you couldn't bear to be apart from her. You left the banquet for me to eat. Be the passionate lover she knows. When she has fallen asleep, take off her rings, bracelets and necklaces and put them in a sack along with all her other jewellery. Before you leave, mark her on the left thigh with the trident. Return here at once with the jewels.'

The prince did exactly as instructed. He made love to the princess and when she slept, he stole her jewels and marked her thigh with the trident. He returned to the house where he and the minister's son were staying and showed him the jewels.

Buddhisena then untied his hair, took off his clothes, rubbed clay all over his body and dressed himself in a simple loincloth as a wandering ascetic. He had the prince do likewise and pretend to be his disciple. They went to a charnel ground and, amid rotting corpses and smouldering bodies, sat beside a burning pyre as if in meditation. When they both smelled of smoke and death, the minister's son whispered to the prince: 'Go now to the market and sell these jewels. When someone recognizes them, say that I am your guru. I gave them to you. Bring the accusers to me.'

'The prince took the bag of jewellery to a goldsmith whose shop was near the king's palace gate. The goldsmith immediately recognized the jewels and summoned the palace guard. 'These belong to the princess,' he shouted as a crowd gathered.

The disguised prince explained they belonged to his guru who wanted him to sell them. He had no idea how they had come into the possession of the great yogi. The palace guards, accompanied now by the goldsmith, his assistants and a crowd of men and women, went with the disguised prince to the charnel ground. There they seized the so-called yogi and, bringing the sack of jewels as evidence, went back to the palace so the king might judge this crime.

King Dantāghatā listened carefully as each told his part of the story. Then he asked the yogi: 'Master, tell me where you obtained my daughter's jewellery.'

The ascetic replied: 'Sire, on the last night of the dark lunar fortnight, I was sitting in the charnel ground doing secret practices to strengthen the seductive powers of a woman, a yogini who had asked for my help. She came to me at midnight and gave me her jewels and robes. Then I made offerings and sang prayers to the Great Goddess, while this woman stood naked before me. To complete this ancient rite, I took a trident and made three lines on her left thigh. She let me keep the jewels to pay for my services.'

The king said he would issue his judgement next day. The yogi returned to the charnel ground, and the king, now full of apprehension, returned to his apartments. There he asked the queen: 'Go see if princess has a mark on her left thigh and if she does, tell me what kind of mark.'

The queen went to her sleeping daughter, inspected her leg and asked the drowsy girl what this mark was. The princess had no idea. The queen returned and told the king: 'Indeed, my lord, there is a mark on Padmāvatī's left thigh. Three parallel lines as if she had been marked with a trident. But sire, she says she has no idea how such a mark came to be there.'

Dantāghatā went cold and was silent. Then he summoned his guards and had them bring the yogi, who of course, was Buddisena, from the charnel ground. When the ascetic had arrived and stood before him, the king asked: 'You are wise, a guru, are you not?'

The yogi bowed and assented. 'If a woman in one's household has become a shameless creature and has acted outside the bounds of decency, what did the sages of the past consider the proper way to proceed?'

The fake guru considered and then replied: 'Your Majesty, it is said in all the scriptures that if a Brahmin, a cow, a wife, a child or any other household member brings disgrace to the master's house, that person or being should forever be put out, expelled, sent away, banished, exiled.'

'So be it,' said the king.

The king loved Princess Padmāvatī. She had been his favourite daughter, but now he could not bear to see her again. He didn't want her in his mind for another second. He would no longer speak her name. He commanded that this terrible child be placed in a palanquin and taken immediately to the wilderness outside his kingdom's border. The guards were neither to explain nor speak to her. So, they were silent as they took her away from her weeping attendants and put her in a plain wooden litter with canvas sides. Quickly, they soon left the great city of Karnakubja far behind.

Princess Padmāvatī saw that this was not her usual palanquin with its brocade panels and scented pillows. She was being punished. Her desperate plot to poison the prince's friend had succeeded and must have been discovered. Her father, the king, had somehow learned of both her murderous plot and her tumultuous passion for the prince. Padmāvāti knew she had lost everything and was in utter despair. How could she have been so rash? But how could she have done otherwise? Surely, she was being taken to the execution ground. She called out to ask the bearers where they were taking her, but they did not reply. The litter shook and jostled as the soldiers, smelling of sweat and cursing at each obstacle, manhandled it through the jungle. Tree shadows flickered on the cloth roof. The princess wanted to weep but would not let herself. Her memories of her life before this moment seemed a dream. Then the guards stopped and the bearers set down the palanquin. No one said a word, but she heard them leave. They had left her in the jungle all alone. She had no idea what fate would now bring. She dared not move.

Prince Vajramukuta and Buddhisena had followed the furtive procession as it carried the princess from the city. They waited in the forest until the guards and porters were long gone. When they rode up to the palanquin, the princess pulled the curtains aside. When she saw the prince and his friend, she did not know whether to be relieved or terrified. Did the prince know? His companion surely did. He was alive. Had her father decided to let the prince take his revenge and kill her? She looked up into the prince's eyes. It was clear he knew what she had planned. Would he kill her? He had every right. How could they ever forgive her?

She saw that he was undecided and was paralysed with fear. The prince's hand was on his sword but he too couldn't move. Then the minister's son said: 'All the wise agree, My Lord: love brings more joy to the living than the dead.'

The prince nodded and gestured for Padmāvatī to get up on his horse behind him. She reached around his waist. He did not flinch. The heat of her body, her scent, slowly had their effect on him. When they reached the prince's kingdom, the king and queen were overjoyed to see that he had found such a beautiful and entrancing wife. They were glad to see him happy. The two were married and lived a life of lasting bliss.

'Did you like the story?' asked the corpse-spirit in his disembodied whisper.

The king shrugged and felt the cold cloud of dampness shift on his shoulder. The Vetāla continued: 'All those who took part in this drama will have died by now. And it is Yama, Lord of the Dead, who decides who gets a better rebirth and who a worse one.'

King Vikramāditya nodded. 'And as a king yourself, you must be accustomed to rendering such judgements, so answer this. Who of the five people in this tale—the prince, his friend, the princess, her nurse, King Dantāghatā—merits the lowest rebirth?'

King Vikramāditya knew but tried not to speak. A terrible pulsing pain burst behind his eyes and seemed to fill his brain. The more he tried not to answer, the more the pain's violence increased. It began to feel as if his brain were boiling. Finally, to stop the pain, he answered, 'The prince and the princess both fulfilled their desires and assumed the place in life to which they had been born. Both did what fate and convention required. The minister's son was unswerving in working to satisfy his master's needs. He behaved correctly. The old nurse also served her former mistress as duty required. But King Dantāghatā, Padmāvatī's father, should never have judged her without questioning her directly. This was unjust. He deserves the lowest rebirth.'

As King Vikramāditya finished the word 'rebirth', the Vetāla vanished.

STORY 2

Three Suitors

King Vikramāditya walked back through the damp, dripping forest until again he came to the charnel ground and the tree where the corpse-spirit hung. He climbed up and cut down the Vetāla. It fell to the ground like a feather. The king picked up the corpse and swung it onto his shoulder. Again, he felt the damp chill on his skin. Together, they began the journey back to where the yogi waited. After a while, the Vetāla murmured:

'O Great King, I am honoured that you deign to carry such an unfortunate being as I. Never did I imagine that I would rest on royal shoulders.' It paused as if waiting, then sighed. 'Well, here's another story which may interest you.'

The corpse-spirit, its voice like a cold draft, began.

Famed for its three turquoise towers, Dharamasthala was a prosperous city on the banks of the Jumna, and King Gunādhipa's reign there was a time of great scholarly and spiritual attainments. Among his distinguished subjects were a Brahmin priest, Keśava; the priest's wife; his son, a promising scholar; and his beautiful, clever daughter, Mandaravatī. Mandaravatī had just reached the age of womanhood and her family was anxious to find her a husband who would enhance its lineage and reputation. One day, when her father was away performing rites and her brother was off studying in the city, a handsome, serious and well-spoken young Brahmin named Tribikram happened by the house and asked for a cup of water. Mandaravatī's mother saw that he could make an excellent husband for her daughter. She invited him in and, after chatting for a while, asked Mandaravatī to join them. The girl found the young Brahmin appealing. Without hesitating, the mother proposed that the two should marry. Tribikram quickly agreed. He left to get his parents' approval and promised he would return the next day to formalize matters.

That evening, Keśava returned home and announced that he had just found a suitable husband for Mandaravatī. He was a Brahmin named Barnan, well-educated, sincere, of excellent family and suitable in every way. He would visit them the next day.

No sooner had Késava finished than Mandaravatī's brother returned and made a similar announcement. Tomorrow, this prospective husband, a well-born, wealthy and learned Brahmin named Madhusudan, would come to the house. At that point, Keśava, his wife, his son and Mandaravatī all looked at each other in consternation. Keśava thought to himself: 'One daughter? Three suitors? Each of us has given our word. Now whom shall I choose and whom do I reject? I cannot avoid offending two important families. I'll look like an utter fool. What shall I do?'

The next day the three suitors arrived, dressed in their finest, and stood in a row in front of the house. Keśava sat before them on the front porch, completely undecided. His wife busied herself making tea. Mandaravatī wanted to escape the ridiculous scene that was sure to follow and went into the garden. All the suitors were equally well-born, handsome and educated. How could she choose? Could she end up with three husbands? she wondered. Draupadi, heroine of the Mahabharata, had five. So, it was possible.

She was distracted by these musings when a long black cobra slid from under the rose bushes and suddenly bit her on the heel. She gave a cry that sounded more surprised than frightened, fell to the ground and, before anyone could come, she died.

Keśava, his wife, son and the three suitors all heard her cry out and ran into the garden. Though Mandaravatī was certainly not alive, her parents and brother insisted that still she might be saved. A skilled doctor, snake handler or yogi could draw the poison from her body and then she just might live. They raced through the neighbourhood and each found such a master, but all agreed that Mandaravatī could not be revived. The experts could only give the same advice: 'Dear sirs, dear madam, even Lord Brahma cannot conquer death. Now you can only perform funeral rites, cremate her and set her free from the sorrows of this world.'

They accepted their fees and left. Keśava did as they advised, and when his daughter's body had been sent to the cremation ground, his wife and he shut themselves in their house to pray.

The three suitors, heartbroken and in despair, remained by Mandharavatī's pyre at the charnel ground. Then the first suitor, Tribikram, collected Mandaravatī's bones and placed them in a sack. He walked into the forest and afterwards lived as a mendicant, carrying the bones wherever he went. The second suitor, Barnan, swept up her ashes and put them in a box. He kept them near him in a hut in the charnel ground where he continued to live. The third suitor, Madhusudan, became a devotee of Viśnu and, dressed in the rags of a sadhu, went from pilgrimage place to pilgrimage place. All remained obsessed with the woman they had hoped to marry.

Many years later, Madhusudan was wandering in the countryside when he came upon the compound of a wealthy Brahmin. He knocked at the gate, asked for food and was invited in. After he washed his face, hands and feet, he was seated next to his host in the dining room adjoining the kitchen. The Brahmin's wife served them bowls of rice, lentils and curried vegetables. Meanwhile, her child kept whining and nagging and demanding that she feed him again. The child clung to her skirt and tried to pull her away. This went on and on until the Brahmin's wife lost her temper. She picked up the child and hurled him into the kitchen fire. The child screamed and thrashed in the burning coals; he knocked over a jar of oil, which blazed up and burned until he was a blackened corpse. His mother looked on as if all this were normal.

Madhusudan was horrified and stood up to leave. 'Why haven't you eaten? Aren't you hungry?' asked his host, surprised to find his hospitality rejected.

'How can anyone stay where such a terrible thing has taken place?' replied Madhusudan. The Brahmin, without another word, left the room, returning with a red wooden box. He took out six turquoise talismans and a book. He placed the talismans around the child's charred body, opened the book, whispered into the child's ear, and chanted for half an hour. Then a dark whirlwind appeared out of nowhere, lifted the body off the ground and seemed to consume it. Then, as suddenly as it began, the whirlwind vanished and there was the little boy, as alive as before, without the slightest scar or mark on his body. The child seemed dazed, but after the Brahmin reminded him where he was, he became himself again and, as if nothing had happened, laughed and ran off to play in the garden.

Madhusudan wondered whether, if he had such a text and such talismans, would it not be possible to bring Mandaravatī back to life? He resumed his meal and asked the Brahmin if he might stay for a few days longer. The Brahmin nodded hospitably, and the two spent the next few days conversing about spiritual matters and eating together.

On the third night, when everyone was fast asleep, Madhusudan slipped into his host's room and stole the red box. He ran through the forest, stopping only to catch his breath and, within a week, reached the cremation ground where Mandaravatī's body had been burnt. There, in his hut, was Barnan, and with him, Tribikram, who happened to be visiting.

'Brothers!' Barnan cried. 'Surely, after so many years, fate has brought us together for a purpose.'

'Tell us about your travels,' said Tribikram to Madhusudan. 'What teachings have you received? What have you learned?'

And so, though he did not explain how he had come by such magic, Madhusudan told them that he had learned how to bring the dead back to life. They decided, then and there, to revive Mandaravatī.

'We have, each of us, longed for her for so long,' they agreed. Tribikram piled the bones on the ground. Then Barnan heaped the ashes around them. After that, Madhusudan placed the turquoise talismans around the remains. He addressed the heap of bone and ash with Mandaravatī's name, opened the book and chanted for half an hour just as he had heard done before. A scarlet whirlwind appeared out of nowhere, lifted the bones and ash off the ground, and they disappeared. The wind continued to spin violently until suddenly it ceased. In the stillness, there before them sat Mandaravatī, lustrous and beautiful as before.

The three men all wept and then laughed. But soon they began to argue about who should marry her. They could not agree, and their quarrelling became evermore angry while Mandaravatī, the woman they all loved, looked on in a state of vacant confusion.

'Great King …' asked the Vetāla in its ghostly whisper. 'O Great Judge of Men, tell me … who was actually entitled to be the husband of this unfortunate woman?'

The answer was as clear to Vikramāditya as the sun emerging from behind a cloud. Immediately, he felt a bolt of lightning cut into his brain and he answered before he could even think to stop himself, 'She is the wife of Barnan, who built the hut and stayed with her ashes.'

'But if Tribikram had not preserved her bones,' the Vetāla whispered, 'she could not live … and if Madhusudan had not learned how to bring her back to life, she could not live. Each did something necessary. So, why Barnan?'

King Vikramāditya felt the pain in his head abate and he continued: 'Tribikram preserved Mandaravatī's bones; he cared for them just as a good son takes care of his mother. But a son cannot marry his mother and since he has acted as her son, he is ineligible to marry Mandaravatī. Then there is Madhusudan. Indeed, he brought Mandaravatī back to life, but in doing so, he acted as a father. Just as the father gives the seed that produces the child, Madhusudan gave the seed syllables, the essence that produced life. By every law and convention, he also cannot marry her. In the end, only Barnan is free of such ancient prohibitions. Only he is eligible to marry Mandaravatī.'

'Subtly argued,' whispered the corpse-spirit as it slid away. It flew back to the tree and immediately was again hanging amid the phosphorescent leaves. The king raced behind. He climbed the tree, cut down the Vetāla, put it over his shoulder. A chill penetrated his skin from the dankness of the demon's form. Again, he began his journey to meet the yogi in the charnel ground.

STORY 3

Service

'Stories are better than walking in the dark,' the corpse-spirit whispered. 'O King, may I tell you another one?'

King Vikramāditya shrugged, jostling the chilly cloud-like form on his back. The Vetāla paused before beginning.

One afternoon not very long ago, in the yellow-gated city of Vardhamāna, King Śūdraka, a possessive man, was taking his ease in his apartments near the palace gates. He heard the loud voices of a crowd and called his guard. 'What is that racket? What are those people doing at my gate? What do they want?'

The guard went to investigate and soon returned. 'Great King, every day at this time, people assemble at this gate to ask for money, for favours or for employment. One of your ministers will soon see to their needs.'

King Śūdraka thought, 'A ruler should know the needs of his people.' So, he made a point of resting in the apartment by the gate and listening to the crowd below. Thus, when the king happened to hear a Rajput warrior asking for a place in the palace guard, he looked out. The soldier's clothes were dusty and he looked tired, but he was tall and sunburnt and very muscular.

The king commanded: 'Bring that man to me now.'

When the warrior stood before him, the king asked: 'O Rajput, indeed you look strong. Your demeanour shows you are well trained. What is your name?'

The warrior bowed low and answered: 'I am called Madanavira.'

'And Madanavira, were I to employ you, what would your services cost?'

'O Magnificent One,' the warrior replied. 'My only wish is to serve you. If you pay me a thousand tolas of gold each week, I can properly support myself, my wife, my son and my daughter.'

The courtiers, attendants and guards burst out laughing. This was a gigantic amount of money. But the king's reflections took a different turn. 'Why,' he wondered 'has this man asked for so much? He knows that this is far more than anyone else would ever pay. But if I pay him so extravagantly, he will see I value him more than others ever will. He will serve me with unequalled devotion.'

The king commanded that his treasurer give the Rajput, Madanavira, a thousand tolas of gold for every week he served the king. Madanavira gave half this sum to Brahmins for sacrifices and offerings in the king's honour. A quarter he gave to pilgrims and wandering yogis for the same purpose. An eighth he gave, also in the king's name, for food for the poor and the sick. The final portion of what he earned he used for his family and himself.

Every night Madanavira, armed with sword and shield, would guard the door to King Śūdraka's bedchamber. If the king woke, he would always call out: 'Who attends me now?'

Madanavira would always answer: 'Great King, Madanavira is here. He is yours to command.' And, whatever the king desired, Madanavira saw to it immediately. Never wavering in his vigilance even for a second, he earned his enormous salary. By night or by day, whether eating, drinking, sleeping, sitting still or moving, the king was always on his mind. Madanavira knew that a servant is one who sells himself and when sold, he subordinates all his concerns to his purchaser. He has no more time of his own and no peace of mind. Whether this master is wise or foolish, learned or unlettered, courageous or afraid, a servant must be as silent and watchful as one in the presence of a beast that kills without warning. For this reason, the wise say: 'The duties of a servant serving his master are more difficult than those of a priest serving the gods.'

Once, in the middle of a moonless night, as the king slept and Madanavira stood guard, a woman was heard sobbing loudly in a charnel ground near the forest. Her wailing was like a wild beast in agony. She woke the king. He called out: 'Who attends me now?'

Madanavira, as ever, answered: 'O Great King, Madanavira is here. I am yours to command.'

'Go to the charnel ground. Find out what so distresses the woman who is weeping there. Return at once and tell me.'

When the guard had left, the king said to himself: 'This servant is paid more than all the others. It is time to discover whether he will obey even an unreasonable order. I will learn whether he is loyal or not. And even if he is loyal, I must see whether he is brave or cowardly, ingenious, or stupid.' The king dressed in black and hurried after Madanavira.

When he reached the charnel ground, Madanavira saw, in the darkness, amid the guttering flames of the cremation pyres, a woman, young, dark and slender, naked with flashing diamond bangles, running and dancing in and out of the shadows. She wept and screamed, tore at her hair, was covered with blood as she raked her face and breasts with her long nails. 'No!' she screamed over and over. 'No!'

Madanavira shivered. This was the very image of the Dark One, the Great Destroyer, All-Consuming Lust. He was terrified but forced himself to step forward. 'Who are you?' he asked. 'Why are you weeping? Why harm yourself?'

She stared at him with bloodshot eyes and howled, 'Fool, I am the life force the of this kingdom. I am the power of King Śūdraka and all the kings of Vardhamāna.'

'Then why are you in such despair?' the warrior asked.

The creature cried out, 'Impious, faithless people pollute the good king's realm. It is unbearable. I must go. One month after I leave, the king will be struck down with leprosy and die. This land has been a happy place for me. I weep because I see the future.'

Madanavira was terrified and begged the Goddess: 'What can be done? Can the king escape this fate? I will do anything so my lord may live and prosper.'

The dark woman replied: 'Eight miles to the east, there is a temple sacred to Mahādevī, the Great Goddess who is life and death. If you go there, if you cut off your son's head and offer it to the Goddess, then your king will reign for a hundred years. No evil will affect him.'

After that, the terrifying woman vanished in the smoke.

Madanavira ran home; the king, hidden in the shadows, followed. The guard woke his wife and told her what had happened. Madanavira's son and daughter, roused by their father's unexpected return, heard everything. Their mother called them and spoke to her son. 'O my beloved boy, there is no choice. By sacrificing your head and life, you will save the king and preserve the peace of everyone in his kingdom.'

The son, though only fifteen, did not hesitate. 'Mother, you have taught me that an obedient son, a healthy body, the wisdom to benefit others and a helpful wife are the four things which bring happiness and avert misfortune. You have taught that an unwilling servant, a miserly ruler, an insincere friend and a hateful wife are the four things that destroy peace and guarantee misery. I know the king is my father's master, just as my father is my master. I know what I must do. Mother, first, I will always obey you. Second, I must always be of service to my lord. Third, if my body can be of use to a deity, there is no better fate. Let us go now. Let me serve you and our lord with this sacrifice.'

Madanavira nodded and turned to his wife and son. 'Since, dearest wife, you accept what we must do, and since our son agrees, I will now take him to the temple and sacrifice him.'

His wife replied: 'My final responsibilities are not to my son or daughter, my kinfolk, my mother, or father. My life and happiness are sustained only by you. It is written that a woman's fate is determined not by religious devotions, but by serving her husband, whether he is good or bad, blind, crippled or a leper. It is said that in this world, no matter what kinds of virtuous acts a woman performs, if she does not obey her husband, she will go to hell. I will go with you and my son now.'

Madanavira's daughter began to cry. 'What we must do is terrible, but how can I stay behind when there is no one to care for me?' She accepted that her family's fate would be hers.

Madanavira listened and sighed. Then without further hesitation, he led his family to the temple of the Dark Goddess.

The king followed in secret. Inside the temple, Madanavira stood with his son before the black and terrifying statue of the Great Destroyer. Both sang the deity's praises, then Madanavira joined his hands in supplication. 'O Great Goddess, O you who knows neither shame or regret, who gives birth to the world and devours the world, accept this offering of my son's head and life. Grant that our king live untroubled for his destined years, and that suffering be unknown in his domain.'

With that, Madanavira drew his sword and, with a single stroke, sliced through his son's neck. The boy's head fell to the floor and his blood spurted in all directions.

When the daughter saw her brother's corpse fall to the ground, she wrenched her father's sword from his hand and slit her own throat. Madanavira's wife was overcome with horror at the sight of both her children dead. Without a word, she took the sword and cut her own throat.

Madanavira was stunned to see his family transformed into a heap of twitching corpses in a lake of blood. 'My wife, my daughter, my son are dead. Why must we in this world serve masters if we are to stay alive and support our families? What is the purpose of such a life?' In despair, he seized the bloody sword. He pulled the blade across his neck with such force that he cut off his head.

Hiding in an alcove, the king watched the slaughter. It was all too sudden for him to stop it. He was horrified. He cried out: 'For my sake and my sake alone, this family butchered itself. My rule is a curse on my people. Such terrible, pointless sacrifices make it all too clear: there is no virtue, no goodness, and only boundless cruelty in this world of kings and servants.' Drawing his sword, the king prepared to end his life.

But, at that instant, the statue of the Great Kāli, the Great Mother, black, lustrous, her eyes bloodshot, her mouth in a terrible smile, came to life. She stepped down from the shrine and grasped the king's hand. She spoke in a voice that was strangely tender and melodious: 'O my child. You think what you have just done and seen is terrible. Look at me: life continues by violence and death. But few are willing to sacrifice themselves out of love for their servants. Your compassion and courage have moved me. Whatever you want, I will grant.'

Without hesitating, the king asked that she restore Madanavira and his family to life. Instantly, the Great Black One filled the world with darkness. A hissing sound like a cobra about to strike filed the air. The king and Madanavira found themselves in the temple looking at the warrior's family standing before them smiling, as if nothing had happened. The king wept, overwhelmed by Madanavira's willingness to sacrifice everything he loved.

The next day, in the presence of all his court, soldiers and servants, he gave the warrior half his kingdom.

The Vetāla stopped, but King Vikramāditya strode on steadily through the night. The evening had become strangely warm. The two continued in silence through the dark forest. The only sounds were Vikramāditya's footsteps, the hooting of owls and the slithering of snakes.

The corpse-spirit spoke: 'But in such a ruthless world, tell me: of the five in our story, the warrior Madanavira, his wife, his son, his daughter or King Śūdraka, who was the most virtuous?'

Again, Vikramāditya knew the answer easily; again, his head began to throb, and he answered quickly, 'It is obvious, O Vetāla. Madanavira, his wife and his children did nothing other than what is expected of them and what they expect of themselves. But the king was under no obligation to concern himself with the lives of the many over whom he held sway. Only the king did something truly voluntary, so his virtue was the greatest.'

And, with that, the corpse-spirit evaporated from Vikramāditya's shoulders and returned to where it had hung before. Once again, King Vikramāditya went back to collect it. He cut down the faintly glowing body and slung it across his shoulder. He sighed; this series of events would repeat over and over. His throat was dry. Carrying the Vetāla, he resumed his journey, moving steadily through the dark.

STORY 4

Wise Birds

As King Vikramāditya strode on with his corpse-spirit burden, all that could be heard were the cries of foxes, the snapping of twigs and dew dripping from the leaves The king could barely hear the Vetāla's whisper: 'Great King, I wish I knew stories of a better, happier world, but alas, it's not so. Why, even birds find themselves shocked by what they see here. Listen.'

The Vetāla paused, then began.

Once upon a time, there was a red-walled city called Bhogavati where a kind king named Rūpasena ruled. King Rūpasena owned a handsome emerald-green male parrot named Vidagdhachudāmani. This bird was not only decorative but gifted with wisdom and great eloquence. The king held him in the highest regard and indeed, thought of him not as a pet but as his minister. One day the king asked his parrot: 'O Jewel-like and Far-seeing One, how much do you know?'

The parrot bowed. 'Sire, I know everything.'

'Do you know of a woman, beautiful and equal to me in rank?'

'That's easy,' the parrot replied. 'In the land of the Magadhas, King Magadheśvara's daughter, Princess

Surasandarī, is exactly as you describe. And sire, she is both beautiful and learned.'

When the king heard the princess's name, he instantly fell in love with her. The parrot paused and cocked his head, and blinked. 'Your Majesty, I know something else. Soon, she will be your bride.'

To confirm what he now longed for, King Rūpasena then summoned his astrologer and asked: 'To whom am I fated to be wed?'

The astrologer consulted his charts, inspected the constellations and assured the king that Princess Surasandarī would definitely be his bride. The king was completely overjoyed. He summoned a Brahmin priest to be his emissary and said: 'Go to the king of Magadha. If you succeed in arranging this marriage, I will make you a rich man.'

At the exact same time, in the land of the Magadhas, Princess Surasandarī was talking to her mynah. This bird, glossy obsidian black, exceedingly intelligent and supremely well-spoken, was named Madanamanjarī. The princess relied on her in all things and asked: 'In this wide world, O Wise and Winged One, is there a husband worthy of me?'

The bird answered confidently: 'Dear Princess, King Rūpasena of Bhogavati is worthy of you. He will be your husband.'

And, like a flash of lightning from a cloudless sky, on hearing his name, the princess fell in love with King Rūpasena.

And so, King Rūpasena and Princess Surasandarī fell in love and within two months were united as husband and wife. They lived together in happiness so seamless, it was if they had never been apart.

One day they were sitting in the throne room. King Rūpasena's emerald parrot was in a silver cage to his left, and Queen Surasandarī's obsidian mynah was in a silver cage to her right. The king suddenly had an idea. 'Our joy proves that a life not shared with a loving companion cannot be a happy one.'

'True,' the queen replied.

'Well, since these two birds are so dear to us, we must make every effort to secure their happiness. They should live together as man and wife.'

'An excellent idea,' the queen agreed.

So, they ordered the construction of a much larger silver cage for the two birds. But when the parrot and the mynah were installed in their splendid enclosure, the king and queen could not help but notice that something was wrong. Though the two birds had always been friendly, now they acted like strangers, eyed each other suspiciously and perched as far apart as possible.

One afternoon, the king and queen overheard the parrot as he strutted back and forth on his side of the cage. 'You must know, O Wise Mynah, that in this world it is said that sexual intercourse is the summit of bliss. Many people assert that those who do not experience it have wasted their lives. Now fate has put us in proximity, and the king and queen who own us desire that we live as man and wife. Perhaps then we should copulate and learn to enjoy such transports.'

Without budging from her side of the cage, the mynah answered: 'Kind Parrot, I regret to say that I have absolutely no desire to have sexual intercourse with any male.'

'But why?' the parrot asked.

The mynah answered: 'Dear Gem-like Friend, I am sorry, but I have observed that in every species, those of the male sex are always the most deceitful and predatory, the most violent, the most likely to kill their mate. Surely you have noticed this?'

The parrot was deeply offended and shook his head. 'O Night-winged Mynah, as I have seen, the members of the female sex are certainly no less deceitful, greedy, faithless and are as likely to murder as any male.' And so, the two began to quarrel, both striding back and forth on their perches as they hurled invectives on the opposite sex.

'What is this?' asked the king.

'Why are you quarrelling?' asked the queen.

The mynah came close to the bars of the cage. 'O Great King, O Merciful Queen, we wish to please you, so the parrot proposes to copulate with me, but I do not wish to. I admire his great wisdom and indeed he is beautiful, but I fear him as much as I admire him.'

'But why?' asked the queen.

The mynah replied: 'Your Majesties, all the world knows that it is the male who will dishonour his wife. It is the male who will rape and kill any woman he pleases. Let me tell you a story that makes this transparently clear.'

Shaking with rage, the mynah ruffled her black feathers and began.

'In a city named Elapuram, there lived a rich merchant named Mahādhani whose wives could not produce a child. He yearned for children and went on pilgrimage after pilgrimage, undertook fasts and gave vast sums to Brahmins to recite the Puranas day and night. Finally, his prayers were answered: a son was born. He named his son Dhanakśaya. The merchant celebrated the birth in great style and gave bags of gold coins to Brahmins and chanters, great plates of food and pitchers of wine to the homeless and destitute. He had no more children and gave his only child every advantage. He had him educated by the finest scholars and instructed by the most holy priests. He was trained by the best swordsmen and learned to ride from the most renowned equestrians. But the boy turned out badly. Rather than studying, he gambled and frequented wine shops and whorehouses. His friends and confidants were all idlers and wastrels.

'Mahādhani died without ever realizing his son's true nature. Freed from even the slightest paternal restraint, Dhanakśaya then spent every day drinking and gambling and every night embroiled with prostitutes. He paid his friends' bills and acted like a great lord. In a few years the fortune he inherited was gone and in its place were mountains of debt. With nothing but his clothing, he fled from his creditors and went to the city of Punyavardāna. There he called on an old friend of his late father's, a wealthy merchant named Udbhata. This merchant was delighted to meet his late friend's son and asked how he could have fallen into such desperate straits. Sighing, the shameless son began: "I hired a ship and loaded it with goods. In Ceylon I sold brocades and some very fine sapphires for a good profit. Alas, on the return voyage, a terrible storm destroyed the ship. The captain and all the crew drowned. I alone survived. I clung to a spar and floated on the sea for several days. I have no idea how I survived, but I woke up on a nearby shore and eventually made my way here. Having lost everything, I was too ashamed to return home."

'As the merchant listened, a thought began to dawn: "Great Vishnu, the All-Merciful, has sent this young man to resolve the very problem that has troubled me the most." The merchant doted on his daughter, Ratnavatī. She was very beautiful, but so desperate to marry that she scared men off. The merchant had provided a huge dowry. He had spent a small fortune on prayers and charitable gifts. Until this very moment, all his efforts had been in vain. Here, at last, was a man of excellent family, a perfect match, and a man in no position to decline. Udbhata opened his house to his old friend's son and provided him with a wardrobe and money. Dhanakśaya quickly understood what was expected of him.

'The merchant told his wife, his daughter and his prospective son-in-law, "Life is uncertain. It is best if we arrange this marriage as quickly as possible." And so, it was agreed. An astrologer determined the earliest advantageous time for the nuptials. Priests, musicians, dancers, caterers were hired so the marriage took place in greatest splendour. The merchant and his wife were very happy and the wedded couple were, to all appearances, overjoyed.

'Soon, Dhanakśaya grew restless. His wife and her family bored him. He said to her, "O my heart's delight, I have never known such happiness, but I worry that my friends in Elapuram have heard nothing from me for almost a year. They must be worried. I must return and tell them of my adventures and good fortune."

'"Do you wish me to come with you?" Ratnavatī asked.

"I would like nothing better, but only if your parents agree. I don't wish to take you away from them."

'Ratnavatī's mother said: "Of course, you should be with your husband. It is expected."

'Ratnavatī clung to Dhanakśaya, imploring, 'O my love, let us never be apart.'

'Udbhata gave his son-in-law a small fortune in gold and provided his daughter with a litter, bearers and a female servant. The couple and their entourage soon departed.

'For a few days, the travellers made their way through the deepening jungle until they found themselves in a small clearing. On three sides were the ruined walls of an abandoned monastery with a dried-up well in the centre. It was strangely silent. "We should take care. This is the kind of place where outlaws and demons hide," said Dhanakśaya. "Perhaps you should give me your jewels. Let me hide them in my robe." Ratnavatī nodded and smiled at her husband tenderly. She gave him all her precious ornaments; he smiled back at her and took them. Suddenly he turned away, grasped his short sword, drew it and swiftly slaughtered all four litter-bearers and the maid. He dragged the bodies to the well and threw them in. Ratnavatī was too shocked and terrified to move. Then, without a word, Dhanakśaya struck her with the hilt of his sword, grabbed her by the neck, dragged her to the well and threw her in. He did not look back as he set off on the road to Elapuram, carrying jewels and gold. He was again rich and free to live as he pleased.

'The next day, a mendicant yogi happened to wander down the same jungle path. He heard sobs echoing inside the well. Looking down, he saw, in the shadows, a young woman in bloodstained robes, lying on a heap of corpses. He shouted down to her: "Who are you? What happened?" Ratnavatī wept in relief and cried out to the yogi. She had hoped she would be rescued and had thought for some time about what to say. "I am the daughter of the merchant, Udbhata. My husband and I were attacked by bandits. They killed our bearers and servants. They threw me in this well. They have carried off my husband and all our wealth." After pulling her out of the well, the yogi took her back to her family.

'Bloody, bruised, clothes torn, covered with mud, her face tear-stained, Ratnavatī ran into her parents' arms. "What happened?" they cried. She wept and told them the same story she had told the yogi, and added: "Is Dhanakśaya alive or dead? I don't know." She collapsed, sobbing.

'Udbhata tried to calm her. "Dear One, don't worry. Jewels can be replaced. Servants too. And your husband ... The bandits will demand a ransom. We will pay to get him back."

'Dhanakśaya, however, was back with his friends in Elapuram, determined to make up for lost time. He sold the stolen gold and jewellery and set about drinking, gambling, hiring musicians, dancers and prostitutes on a scale even greater than before. Soon he was again penniless. To replenish his fortunes, he decided to return to his father-in-law. He would tell Udbhata that Ratnavatī, who surely must be dead, had just given birth to a son and so had stayed behind. They would be so delighted at this wonderful news that surely they would give him more money.

'When he arrived at the gate to Udbhata's house, he was shocked to find Ratnavatī standing there, very much alive. He turned to run but she called out, "Husband, stay. There's nothing to fear. I do not care what you have done. I told my father that bandits had robbed us, killed our servants and abducted you. Tell him this; he will not doubt you. He will be happy you are alive. He will give you more gold and jewels than before. I love you. I am your slave."

'The faithless murderer did as his wife proposed and it all went as she promised. Udbhata gave him new robes, more gold, two servants and ordered a feast to celebrate his return. "This, dear son, is your house. Stay as long as you want." Later, after a long night of lovemaking, Ratnavatī fell into a deep and blissful sleep. Dhanakśaya took a knife and cut her throat. He stripped her body, stole all the gold and jewels he could find and returned to the gambling dens and whore houses of Elapuram.'

Weeping, the mynah ended her story. 'I know all this, Your Majesties, because Ratnavatī's mother, Udbhata's wife, was my owner. We mynahs, like parrots, have long lives. I have seen a man with no heart but many appetites slaughter innocent men and women. Your Majesties, I have seen the limitless evil males are capable of. I resolved, long before I came into the queen's possession, never to trust the male of any species.'

The king and queen were stunned by this monstrous story. They looked at each other and then the king turned to his parrot. 'O Parrot, is it possible that, before I owned you, you learned a similar lesson about females?'

The parrot nodded. 'Listen, O King,' he began.

'Sāgaradatta was a wealthy merchant in Kānćanapuram with an eight-year-old son named Śridatta. A fellow merchant in the nearby city of Śripura had a seven-year-old daughter named Jayshri. Mutual respect and affection led the two merchants to unite their families. They held a lavish wedding to marry their two children. Afterwards, each child returned home to be raised by their respective parents. Only on reaching maturity would they live together.

'Śridatta, in the meantime, went off with his father on long trading voyages. He did not see Jayshri for twelve years. In those twelve years, Jayshri became a ravishing beauty. Even so, she was lonely, disconsolate and an ardent reader of love poems. To her attendant, she sighed, "My youth is being wasted. I yearn for the ecstasies the poets sing of. I crave bliss but have no experience."

'"Oh, my dear," her companion, an experienced woman, replied, "don't torment yourself. When the gods are willing, your husband will take you in his arms, and you will know these joys." Other women might have prayed for a husband's swift return, but Jayshri spent her days behind the lattice of her bedroom window, aching with desire, gazing at passersby on the street outside.

One day, a very handsome, muscular young man sauntered past and happened to look up at the window. He saw, in the shadows, Jayshri's avid shining eyes. The two gazed at each other; their hearts were joined. As fire consumes an abandoned house, Jayshri was consumed with longing. She called to her companion. "See that man in front of our gate? I must meet him."

'The attendant ran after the man. She told him: "The daughter of this house wishes to see you in private. It is better if you meet in my home. I will tell you how to get there."

'The young man understood immediately. "I will come tonight," he promised.

'When Jayshri heard the plan, she smiled. "You are a true friend. I will come to your house as soon as I can. Make everything ready."

'Jayshri's companion went home, set out wine and sweetmeats and covered the bed in red satin sheets. When the young man arrived, she gave him a seat by the door. "Wait. I'll tell my mistress you are waiting." She hurried to Jayshri's house. "He must wait a little longer," the girl whispered. "I cannot leave until everyone is asleep."

'At midnight, Jayshri was finally able to steal away; she ran to her friend's house. In the darkness, she saw the man in his seat by the door. Passion transported her. Soon they were twined together, caressing without restraint. It was everything she had imagined. Just before dawn, Jayshri's attendant woke them. The lovers parted, promising to meet that very night at his house not far away. Then, and for many nights to after, Jayshri joined with her lover, revelling in their unbridled desire.

'Not long afterwards, Jayshri's husband, Śridatta, now a handsome, worldly man, returned from his years of travel. He arrived at his father-in-law's house. He had long imagined being with his childhood bride. He had yearned for this. He was sure that Jayshri would be as ardent as he. Her parents were delighted to see Śridatta after so much time, but Jayshri's blood ran cold. "What can I do?" she whispered to her companion. "Every minute, all I desire is my lover. I crave him like water, food, sleep, wealth and air. What should I do with this husband I do not know or want?"

'The lovesick girl got through the day. That night her parents threw a lavish banquet for Śridatta, and then he retired to the room that had been prepared for the married couple. "Go," said her mother. "Do your duty by your husband." 'But Jayshri's face hardened. Her mother, seeing her resistance, spoke sharply. "He is good-looking. He is rich. He is the son of your father's best friend. You have been married to him for twelve years. It is time to be a real wife."

'Jayshri had no choice but to join her husband in their bed, but when he reached for her, she turned away. She lay there silent, rigid, her face turned to the wall. Śridatta thought she must be shy. He sat up and told her of his voyages and how he had longed for her, but she covered her ears and grimaced. The more he spoke softly to her and the more tender his expressions, the more she despised him. He brought out beautiful silks and brocades, splendid jewels he had bought in faraway bazaars, all for her. She wouldn't look at them. Śridatta held out a ruby necklace. Jayshri closed her eyes tight as he put it around her neck. Finally, he was too exhausted to continue. Lying down on the couch, feeling nothing but despair, he fell asleep. Jayshri, however, could not sleep. Her thoughts were of her lover and she longed for his embrace. When she was sure her husband was asleep, she fled. She ran quickly through the night to her lover's bed.

'That night, a thief was prowling in the shadows, looking for someone to rob. He spotted Jayshri hurrying furtively down the street and saw the glitter of her ruby necklace. "What is this rich girl up to?" he wondered. He followed but before he could catch up to her, Jayshri slipped through the door of her lover's house.

'The bedroom was dark. Jayshri's lover lay in bed, completely still. She was seething with lust and threw herself on him, rubbing him, kissing and moaning. She was so consumed, she did not notice that her lover did not respond. Not an hour earlier, as he lay in bed waiting for her, a small black snake, hiding in the mattress, had slithered out and bitten him on the shin. He had died instantly. His body had not yet cooled, and Jayshri was too passionate to notice. The thief, who had climbed up on the windowsill, watched the girl making love to a corpse and could barely muffle his laughter.

'At the same time, a tiny Vetāla was sleeping, hanging upside down in the nearby eaves like a small translucent bat. It was wakened by the thief's laughter and the sounds from the bedroom. When it looked through the window, the Vetāla saw a beautiful young woman trying to make love to a corpse; it was overcome with lust. It flew down and entered the dead lover's body as easily as if sliding between satin sheets. It then thoroughly enjoyed itself as it had sex with the woman throughout the night. When it was finished, and neither the corpse nor the living woman were of any further use to it, out of sheer malice, it bit off the woman's nose, left the lover's body and flew away. The thief watched all this with amazement and returned to wandering the streets before the sun rose.

'Jayshri screamed as her ecstatic transports ended with violent pain. She felt warm blood and the hole where her nose had been, then the coldness of the corpse beneath her. Suddenly she was in hell. Covering her bloody face with a blanket, she staggered to her companion's house. She was unable to explain what had happened. She only knew she had been in love and now was deformed. Her companion saw only one solution. "Ignore your pain. Go back to your husband's room immediately. Wail. Cry. Call for help. Your father and mother, the servants, will all come running. Point at your husband. Tell them: 'Śridatta cut me!'"

'Jayshri did what her friend advised. Her husband was still asleep. She screamed and howled. Soon, her family and servants crowded into the room. They saw her face covered with blood. They saw the bleeding gash in the centre of her face. "What, what have you done?" they shouted at Śridatta. "You must be mad. Why did you cut off Jayshri's nose? Why ruin her beauty?"

'Śridatta was stunned. He could not understand. He covered his face and sobbed.

'Jayshri's father sent for the police. They bound Śridatta and brought him to the court. Told of this terrible crime, the king came at once to judge the case. First, he interrogated Śridatta, who maintained utter ignorance about what had happened and swore he was innocent. Then the king questioned Jayshri. "Your Majesty!" she replied. "You can see what this man has done to me. I could not defend myself. You must avenge me now."

'The king turned back to Śridatta: "How would a just ruler punish you for such a crime?"

'"Sire, O Merciful and Wise, I am innocent but there is nothing to prove it. You must whatever you think is fair." The king sentenced Śridatta to death by impaling and ordered him taken to the execution grounds.

'As it happened, however, the thief had followed Jayshri home. He knew what had happened and, when he saw that an innocent man was about to be killed, he cried out. The king halted the execution. "Who are you?" he demanded. "O Great King, I am a thief, but in every other way, I am an honest man." The thief then told what he had seen. "If what you say is true," the king said, "this woman's nose can still be found in her dead lover's mouth." The police were sent to examine the corpse, and so it was.

'The king released Śridatta immediately and praised the thief for his honesty. He declared that Jayshri was a wanton deceiver, had her hair shaved off and her face blackened with tar. Mounted facing backwards on a donkey, she was paraded through the city and her crimes proclaimed for all to hear.'

'O Magnanimous Ones,' said the green parrot as he bowed to the king and queen, 'I had the misfortune to be owned by this terrible woman. I saw all this with my own eyes. From her I learned that women, as much as any man, are capable of crimes without limit and not worthy of our trust.'

Now the Vetāla whispered in King Vikramāditya's ear: 'O Wise and Courageous King, O Peerless Judge, tell me: whose guilt is greater?' King Vikramāditya shook his head, which had already begun to ache, as the demon went on: 'The dissolute son or the deceitful daughter?'

King Vikramāditya answered as quickly as he could, 'The woman is worse; she recognizes no law or order beyond her lust.'

The corpse-spirit began to dissolve but stopped. 'Forgive me, sire, but I do not understand. The evil man knew right from wrong but, for his amusement, chose to flout all accepted moral constraints. The woman, however, never thought about morality. She simply followed her passion. Was she any more guilty than a lioness on the hunt or a hawk descending on its prey?'

King Vikramāditya was uneasy, but the corpse-spirit was gone.

STORY 5

Three Suitors II

Groggy and tired, King Vikramāditya trudged back to the charnel ground. Again, there was the Vetāla glowing faintly, hanging upside down in the lifeless tree. Again the cold branches to climb, the rope to cut, the corpse fluttering to the ground. All as before and so again: the king and the corpse-demon set off to meet the yogi who had trapped the king in this unending task. And the Vetāla asked: 'O King, shall I distract you with another story?'

King Vikramāditya nodded.

Long ago, in Ujjayanī, a city known for its luxuriant green gardens, when Mahābhala the Envious ruled, there lived a wise man named Haridāsa who often served as the king's ambassador. Haridāsa had a daughter whose extraordinary beauty and brilliance were known throughout the kingdom and beyond; in honour of the Great Goddess, she was named Mahādevī. When Mahādevī grew to marriageable age, Haridāsa asked her what sort of husband she wanted. She replied firmly: 'I want a man who is accomplished in all arts and ways of knowledge. Find me such a man.'

Haridāsa agreed to do his best.

Soon after, King Mahābala summoned Haridāsa. 'I am sending you to the Southern Kingdom where King Harićandra rules. Inquire after his health and welfare; ask him if you might stay a while. While you are there, observe his manner, his court, the walls of his city, the strength of his army, the prosperity of his markets and the satisfaction of his people. When you have learned all you can, return and tell me what you have found.'

Haridāsa bowed and took his leave.

It took him a week to reach the border of King Harićandra's vast domain and another week to reach its capital. Haridāsa met the king and, as instructed, made salutations, offered lavish gifts of brocade, jewels and learned texts and asked for accommodation. King Harićandra gave him the use of a pleasant residence adjoining the king's sprawling pink marble palace.

One day, King Harićandra summoned Haridāsa before him. 'O wise one,' he asked, 'tell me this. If history passes through four ages—Gold, Silver, Bronze and Iron—are we in the last of these? Is this the time of decline, corruption and vice?'

Haridāsa put his hands together at his chest, bowed and replied: 'Yes, Great King, this is the final age of this cycle. We have moved from the Age of Gold, a time of brilliance, wisdom, compassion and joy, through ages where humanity has slowly fallen into ignorance and sleep. Now is a time of darkness and dream. People think it wisdom to take advantage of others less able. Order is arbitrary. There is no morality. Violence is pervasive. Self-satisfaction is virtue. The young mock the old. Businessmen rob the sick and dying. People are dazzled by possessions and enslaved by things. Chaos is everywhere. Yes, sire, this is indeed the end of time, the Iron Age.'

Having heard this, the king returned to his quarters and Haridāsa went back to his house.

Soon after, a handsome young Brahmin who had been deeply impressed by Haridāsa's speech came to him. 'Wise emissary,' he said, 'I have something to request of you.'

Haridāsa nodded.

'It is said that you have a daughter of great intelligence and beauty. I would be honoured for her to be my wife.'

Haridāsa replied: 'My daughter will only wed an accomplished and learned man. I promised her this.'

'Sir, I have studied the Vedas and śastras. I am also skilled in practical things.'

'Show me,' Haridāsa asked 'Let me see that what you say is true.'

The Brahmin's son smiled confidently. 'Sir, I have made a magic cart that can transport you anywhere instantly.'

'Can you bring it here tomorrow?' Haridasa asked.

The Brahmin's son did so. Haridāsa was impressed by the gilded chariot and, when the two had stepped in, asked to visit his home in Ujjayanī. The chariot rose in the air; the journey of two weeks took barely five minutes.

Haridāsa invited the young Brahmin into his house and introduced him to his wife and son. They were surprised and strangely embarrassed.

'What is it?' Haridāsa asked them.

'O dear Father,' said the son, 'in your absence, I wished to help fulfil your promise to my sister. I met a good-looking and upright young Brahmin who said he would like to marry her. I told him that she would accept him only if he was accomplished in all forms of knowledge. He said he had such deep mastery of the Upanishads that he could see everything, everywhere in the past, present and future. He then predicted that you would arrive here today. I said that if that took place, Mahādevī was his. Now, Father, you are here, and he is here, waiting to be married.'

Haridāsa turned to his wife. 'Two suitors? Impossible!!'

But she burst out, 'O Husband, it's worse than that. While you were absent and our son was out finding a husband for our daughter, so was I. At the market, I met an extraordinary young Brahmin who wished to marry Mahādevī. I told him her conditions, and he said that he had exceptional command of the Puranas. He was also accomplished in martial arts. He promised he could shoot an arrow and hit anything even if he only heard it. Well, without a second thought, I agreed to accept him for our daughter. He too is here.'

'One daughter. Three husbands!' Haridāsa was at a loss. He thought, 'Even an excess of good qualities brings its own downfall. Sītā was exceedingly beautiful, so Rāvana, the ruler of Lanka, abducted her. Rāvana's skills in battle did not allow him to see that Rāma, whose wife he had stolen, could kill him, but in the end, that is what happened. My daughter's virtues have brought three husbands. What am I to do?'

Haridāsa went to bed and fell into a troubled sleep. That night, while all in the household slept, a rākśasa, a mountain demon, blue-black, iron-toothed, flew above the city, looking down on its citizens as if he were watching shoals of minnows in a shallow pond. He saw Mahādevī asleep, breathing softly, and immediately was consumed with envy that a being should be so beautiful and so desirable. He flew through her window and carried her off to his crystal palace on Kalumar Peak. Mahādevī did now wake but thought she was dreaming.

When morning came and Mahādevī could not be found, no one could imagine what had happened. Haridāsa was at his wits' end. He summoned the three suitors and asked the second suitor, the one who could see all in the past, present and future, where his daughter might be found. He responded: 'Undoubtedly, a mountain demon who dwells on the highest peak in the Vindhya range looked down and saw her. He came and took her to his palace.'

To this, the third suitor, the one most skilled in archery, said: 'I will go and kill this demon and bring you daughter back.'

And the first suitor said to the archer: 'Use my magic cart. Go the mountain, kill the demon and return with her.'

The archer did so. He rode in the cart to the rākśasa's palace, shot an arrow through the monster's eye and killed him. Then he brought Mahādevī back to her family.

No sooner had Mahādevī returned and retired to her quarters than the three suitors began to quarrel over who was her rightful husband. Haridāsa shook his head. 'What am I to do? My daughter and I both have an obligation to each of these men. All are accomplished in their way. Whom should I choose to be her husband?'

The Vetāla paused. 'O Wisest of Kings …' King Vikramāditya shivered as the ghostly breath touched his ear. '… which of these three, who should Haridāsa choose as Mahādevī's spouse?'

Already the king felt his head throbbing. He spoke quickly: 'If all the suitors are equally learned, the one who slew the demon and returned Mahādevī to her father's house should become her husband.'

'And why so, O King?' the corpse-spirit asked. 'After all, without the clairvoyance of one suitor and the remarkable cart invented by the other, Mahādevī could not have been saved.'

The king explained: 'Certainly, Haridāsa was obliged to reward both these men. But these were favours that those two suitors could easily grant. However, the suitor who fought the demon risked his life. He did not know the nature of the demon's power or skill. He might easily have been maimed or killed. He took the greatest risk and thus he earned the right to marry Mahādevī.'

'How easily that came to you,' the Vetāla hissed merrily. 'Kingship must have given you practice in rendering swift judgement.'

The corpse-spirit slipped away. In his mind, before he had even taken a step, King Vikramāditya could already see the Vetāla at the end of a rope, swinging slowly from the top branch of the tree in the charnel ground.

STORY 6

Transposed Heads

Again, King Vikramāditya climbed the tree where the Vetāla hung. It seemed to take more effort. He cut the rope. The corpse-spirit floated to the ground. The king flung the cold phosphorescent thing over his shoulder and returned to the familiar path. Soon, the corpse-demon spoke in his sibilant, faintly mocking voice. 'Well, here's another tale, O King. Perhaps it will distract you for a while.'

The Vetāla began.

In Bengal, there was a city named Dharmadpuramī, with streets paved in white marble. The king, Dharmaśila, was easy-going. One day, he said to his minister Andhak: 'Only one thing prevents me from being completely happy and my kingdom from being secure. I have no heir.'

Andhak considered and replied: 'O King, the śastras and all the wise agree: the Great Goddess, Mahādevī, the Wrathful Mother of life and death, has the power to shape and reshape our fate. If you build a temple of unequalled splendour with an altar to house her image and if you make offerings and chant praises before her, the Great Goddess will surely grant your wish.'

King Dharmaśila accepted his minister's suggestion and built a magnificent temple around a glistening onyx image of the Great Mother. It became his practice that every morning before drinking or eating, he would go to his temple and make offerings of sandalwood, rice, flowers, perfume, oil lamps and consecrated food. He would chant many verses of praise to the Goddess. He repeated this month after month, and his practice did not waver.

One morning, as the sun was rising, a young woman's voice, seductive and terrifying, filled the air around him. 'O King,' she said. 'You have pleased me in many ways. Whatever you wish for, I will grant.'

Trembling, the king replied: 'O Mother of my heart, my life, my realm, may it please you to grant me a son.'

The Goddess replied: 'It shall be as you wish.'

Nine months later, the king's favourite consort gave birth to a son. Thereafter, the king's devotion and the Goddess's reward became a famous story. The temple became renowned far and wide as a place where the Great Mother would fulfil the wishes of all who promised their devotions and made offerings to her there.

Years had passed when a laundryman named Dhruva was walking past the Devī's temple. It glittered like a diamond in the sunlight and the laundryman was dazzled. He vowed that one day he would go there and prostrate before the Goddess. An hour later, he saw a willowy young girl of extraordinary beauty walking down the road towards him. She was carrying a large bundle of freshly washed clothing, so he knew that her family must also be laundrymen. He asked her name and where she lived; shyly, she told him. Their eyes met. He felt his heart fly out of his chest and he fell in love. Delirious with love, he raced into the temple and threw himself down before the Dark Goddess. Joining his hands at his heart, he prayed 'O Mother of us all, you create and devour us. By your power and love, allow me to marry the girl I just saw. Life without her is worthless. I will even cut off my head and give it to you if you grant my wish.' Still burning with passion, he made more prostrations before returning home.

He resumed the gruelling routine of washing clothes, but the memory of the girl and her dark-eyed glance tormented him. Unable to sleep, drink or eat, he became more and more exhausted. Day and night, he couldn't stop thinking: 'Who was she? What was she doing? Had she forgotten him? Was she in love with someone else?' His friend saw him wasting away, barely able to work, so he went to Dhruva's father. He told the father that his son had fallen in love. The father smiled and said: 'Oh, he must marry the girl. I will ask around. I'm sure I can find her.'

Since they were all in the same trade, it did not take long to find the girl in a nearby village. The marriage was arranged and soon the two were married. Their life together was a happy one; their business prospered; his wife gave birth to two sons and one daughter. Dhruva could not believe how happy he was.

Ten years later, Dhruva, his wife and his friend were walking in the cool of a summer evening when they found themselves near the temple of the Great Goddess. Dhruva suddenly remembered his terrible vow and was overcome with fear. 'For years, we have been so happy only because of the Wrathful One's blessings. But I forgot my vow. I never considered fulfilling it. I have known her favour. I can't escape her fury. She can and she will destroy me and those I love.'

Dhruva had never known such terror. He said to his wife and his friend, 'I have just remembered that I promised to make a prayer to the Devī. Don't wait for me. I'll make an offering and then catch up to you.' So saying, he went into the temple, bathed and cleansed himself in the pool at the entrance and stood before the image of the Devī with her black sinuous body, her laughing eyes, razor teeth and bloodstained lips. Dhruva knew she could kill everyone he loved with a glance. To her, it was nothing. He prayed and offered praises.

He begged for mercy. Then, with a sword from the shrine, he severed his neck. His head fell to the floor as his body collapsed in a pool of blood.

Soon, his wife and friend began to worry. They had waited for an hour, and there was no sight of him. 'Don't worry,' said his friend. 'I will go back and get him. Wait here. I'm sure everything is all right.'

Dhruva's friend walked back to the temple. There, on the floor in a pool of dark blood, he saw the body and nearby, Dhruva's head. From her place on the shrine, the Goddess smiled at him. He was paralysed at the sight and thought: 'People will think that I killed him because I coveted his wife. No matter what I say, that's the story they'll believe. His family will kill me. My family will be cast out.' He saw no way to escape this, so he went and cleansed himself in the pool, stood before the Devī and prayed. Then he picked up the sword and, with a violent slash, cut off his own head.

Waiting alone by the road, the wife soon began to worry. Something was wrong, she was sure, and she hurried to the temple. She was horrified to see the two bodies lying on the floor in pools of blood. 'My husband's parents, his friend's parents, even my father and mother, will never believe I am innocent. They will make up some story or other. They will say that I encouraged our friend to kill Dhruva because he was my lover and I killed him because I am a lustful woman and craved someone else.' So, she bathed in the temple pool, stood before the Devi, hands folded at her heart, and prayed to the Goddess. She was just about to slit her throat when the Great Wrathful One stepped down from the shrine and seized her arm. In a voice like a bell, the Goddess spoke: 'How could I not be pleased with you, my three devotees, all so willing to sacrifice yourselves. I will grant whatever you desire.'

Dhruva's wife begged that the Great Goddess restore her husband and their friend to life. 'I will,' said the Devī. 'Place their heads back on their bodies.'

Lost in a fog of horror and confusion, Dhruva's wife did her best to obey. The Black Goddess rose in the air like a thundercloud and rained the water of life on the two corpses. Immediately, as droplets hit the bodies, the cloud vanished, the Goddess became again an immobile statue and the temple was silent. Dhruva's wife looked on in a daze as the two men struggled to stand. None of them could make sense of what they saw, but the wife understood first and she screamed. She had accidentally placed the friend's head on her husband's body and her husband's head on their friend's corpse. The two men looked at each other. One nightmare had been replaced by another. Bewildered, each kept touching himself, trying to reconnect with the unfamiliar body he now inhabited. Weeping, Dhruva's wife confessed that before the Goddess restored them to life, it was she who had placed the wrong head on the wrong body. 'This is my fault. Seeing you both dead and headless, I lost my mind,' she sobbed. 'Now, one of you has my husband's head and the other his body.'

When the two realized their situation, they immediately began arguing over who was her rightful husband. She wept as they shouted at each other and began wrestling on the ground.

All was silent. The corpse-spirit laughed. King Vikrāmaditya had been so involved with the story that he was surprised to be back in his world of night wandering. 'Now, O Wise King Vikramāditya, how is this to be resolved? Who is now the husband and who is not? Answer please.'

Before the king's head could throb, the answer was clear. 'Hear, O Demon, it is written in the Vedas: the Gangā is the ruler of all rivers; Mount Sumeru is the lord of all mountains; the Wish-Granting Tree is the king of trees; the head is the ruler of a human being. This woman is the wife of the man who has her husband's head.'

'Of course.' The Vetāla sighed, vanishing in the dark.

STORY 7

Four Suitors

Again, the king was walking through the night with the Vetāla lying across his shoulders like a snow cloud on a mountain. Again, it was whispering, telling a story.

O King, even now, Ćampakā is a blue-walled and prosperous city, as it was when it was ruled by a clever king, Ćampakésvara, and his queen, Sulоćana. Their daughter, Tribhuvansundarī, was a girl of ravishing beauty. Her face was like the moon and her hair was like raven's wings; her lips were like coral and her teeth like pearls. Her waist was like a leopard's, and she moved like palm fronds swaying in a midnight breeze. As she grew into womanhood, her beauty increased daily.

When she reached womanhood, the king and queen began to worry about finding her a worthy husband. Everyone knew that the princess was so beautiful that any man who saw her, whether a prince, a commoner or a forest yogi, would become intoxicated. All the nearby kings had heard of the girl. After having their sons' portraits painted, each had a Brahmin bring the portrait to King Ćampakésvara. The king showed all these royal likenesses to his daughter, but none appealed to her.

The king told the princess, 'Soon you must choose a husband. It is expected of you and it is necessary. Let all the suitors come in person and choose one of them.'

Princess Tribhuvansundarī refused. 'Father,' she said, 'you must give me to a man who has no equal in at least one of three qualities: great beauty, great strength and great knowledge.'

The king agreed.

Few princes wished to be judged by such exacting standards, and only four had the courage to present themselves. The princess sat behind a screen and watched as her father questioned them. To each the king said: 'You know the princess's requirements. State your qualifications.'

The first suitor said: 'O sire, I know how to weave a special kind of cloth. Each bolt sells for five bars of gold. One gold bar I donate to the gods; the second I give to the Brahmin priests. The third is made into a chain I wear around my neck; the fourth I save to give my future wife; and I use the fifth to pay my living expenses. No one in the world knows how to make this cloth, and I am strong enough lift ten bolts by myself. And as to my good looks, you can see me clearly.'

The second suitor said: 'I, O Great King, have learned to speak the languages of the animals and birds, whether they live on the earth, on the sea or in the air. No one else can do this. My strength is unsurpassed. My beauty is before your eyes.'

The third suitor stood to make his case: 'I, O Magnificent One, comprehend all texts, whether sacred or secular, ancient or modern, poetry or prose. I have no equal whatsoever. My body, as you see, is strong, and my appearance, obviously, beautiful.'

The fourth suitor said: 'O Great King, I am unexcelled in my knowledge of weapons and their usage. No one can match me.

With an arrow, I can strike any target, even if I merely hear it. With my sword, I can cleanly slice a crystal glass in two. My beauty is world-renowned; you can see why.'

When the king had heard each suitor, he reflected: 'Each of these men is, in his way, peerless. Which of them should my daughter marry?' When he asked his daughter, she was as much at a loss as he. She hung her head in silence.

With this, the Vetāla had reached the end of his tale. 'O Wise King Vikramāditya, which suitor is the right husband for this beautiful princess?'

At first the king felt no pain, but the torment returned as soon as he found the answer. He spoke quickly. 'O Vetāla, it is clear. The first suitor is clever but obviously of the Sūdra caste, a labourer. The second, the one who knows the languages of birds and beasts is a Bais, a Rajput, suited at best to be a supervisor. The third is clearly a Brahmin. Only one of that caste could be so learned. The last is of the Kśatriya caste, a warrior. This is also the caste of rulers and kings. He alone is suited for the princess to marry.'

The Vetāla paused. 'So, O King, if all other qualities are equal, the decisive factor in the princess's choice must be social caste?'

'Of course,' the king replied. 'She should not be swayed by some kind of intangible allure.'

'Not love at first sight?'

'The marriage of a princess is much more serious than mere attraction.'

With that, the corpse-spirit vanished as if it had never been there at all. The king went again, cut it down, put it on his shoulder; the two began their journey as if for the first time.

STORY 8

Gratitude

Now, locusts and crickets filled the night air with the sound of whirring. The king could barely hear the corpse-spirit's voice as it spun a new tale.

O Wise and Courageous King, the city of Mālavati, famed for its hundred gilded domes, once was ruled by a proud and daring king named Gunādipa. One day, Chiramdeva, a young Rajput warrior of noble bearing, arrived at the palace. He had made the long journey from his homeland in the foothills of the Himalaya and wished to enter King Gunādipa's service. He came daily to the palace gates, hoping to catch the king's attention when the latter rode out hunting. And every day, he was ignored. Within a year, he ran through almost all his money.

Chiramdeva spent the last of savings to buy silk robes, a brocade jacket and an unusually fine bay horse. In such a splendid outfit, he would seem entitled to ride with the king and his courtiers as they went hunting. And indeed, no one objected when he joined the royal party and rode close to the king as he cantered at breakneck speed deep into the forest. Chiramdeva alone dared to stay close when the king swerved up onto a narrow path and lost his courtiers completely.

After a few hours, they reached a small clearing and the king stopped. The Rajput called out: 'Your Majesty, all your attendants have taken another trail. I will be honoured to see to your needs.' He rode up to the king, who looked at him carefully. 'Why, though you have a fine horse, ride well and are dressed as a courtier, are you so very haggard and thin?'

Chiramdeva replied: 'My father abandoned me at birth and never thought of me again. An uncle raised me, but when he died, there was no money and I had to sell his small farm. Now the one whom I would serve has not yet seen me for what I am. He cares for thousands of men, women and children. He is too concerned with others to take care of me among so many.'

The king then understood that this man wished to serve him and listened as he continued, 'Sire, I will serve you perfectly, but I will not beg. I was taught that there are six things that make a man contemptible in others' eyes: first, to have a friend who is a hypocrite; second, to laugh out loud for no reason; third, to fight in public with a woman; fourth, to ride on a donkey; fifth, to speak in a careless or uneducated way; and sixth, to serve a bad master. But, as you also know, Great King, when we are born, fate marks out our length of our life, the kinds of actions we are capable of, the wealth we will enjoy, what knowledge we will be able to acquire and what kind of reputation we will have. O King, one thing in this world is clear: if a man faithfully serves a good master, sooner or later, his reputation will be irreproachable and his livelihood honourable.'

The king listened and understood. At length, he said: 'I'm quite hungry. Could you find me something to eat?' Chiramdeva replied: 'Sire, there is no rice or any kind of grain to be found here. But game must be plentiful.' So he went into the forest and shot a deer, skinned it and cut it up. He gathered wood and leaves, lit a fire and roasted the meat. He then served the king, who had Chiramdeva sit beside him.

When the king was full, he asked: 'Can you find the way back to the city?' Chiramdeva led the king through the forest and when they arrived at the palace, the king made him his principal attendant. He rewarded the Rajput with jewels, robes and an apartment in the palace. Thereafter, Chiramdeva served the king day and night.

One day, the king sent Chiramdeva to inspect a town by the sea, a few days distant. There, on the shore, he came across a small white marble temple set in the centre of a sparkling pool and dedicated to Mahādevī. It shone in the daylight like a luminous pearl. Chiramdeva entered the temple, said prayers and made offerings. As he was leaving, a young woman of extraordinary beauty emerged from the shadows of the shrine. 'Why have you come here, O wanderer?' she asked in a gentle voice.

Chiramdeva bowed and replied, 'This temple is so enchanting, I could not resist. Now your beauty keeps me here.'

The young woman bowed and looked at him flirtatiously. 'If you really want me, first bathe in the pool,' she said. 'Afterwards, I will listen to whatever you propose.'

Immediately, Chiramdeva took off his clothes and immersed himself in the pool. When he climbed out, he suddenly found himself standing naked in the city of his birth near the Himalaya. He was utterly astonished and afraid. Quickly, he put his clothes back on and instantly he was again in front of the temple. The girl was gone. He hurried back to the palace to tell the king what had happened. The king immediately insisted on visiting the temple. They set off on horseback and several days later, they reached the Devi's temple on the shore. They entered, prayed and made offerings. When they emerged, the same young woman greeted them. On seeing the king, she was enthralled; she pledged, on the spot, to obey his every command.

The king smiled and said: 'I command that you become the wife of my faithful servant, Chiramdeva.'

'But sire,' objected, 'it is the splendour of Your Majesty that has captivated me. How could I be the wife of a servant?'

'But,' the king replied, 'did you not pledge to obey whatever I command? You must keep your promise and marry my servant.'

The woman bowed: 'O King, I gave you my heart, so I must obey you. A king's word is law.'

Without ceremony, the king pronounced them married. Chiramdeva and his wife returned to live in the palace of the king.

The Vetāla stopped. The night became still. King Vikramāditya continued walking through the woods. The Vetāla whispered, 'O King, tell me. Whose virtue was greater, the king's or the servant's?'

King Vikramāditya kept moving as he answered.: 'The servant has the greater virtue.'

'How so?' the demon asked. 'Isn't the king's virtue greater? The woman gave herself to him, and he, in turn gave her to his servant as a bride?'

King Vikramāditya replied: 'A king must confer favours on those who serve him. It is neither generosity nor gratitude. He must do so to show he is worthy of their loyalty. But when a servant has subordinated his interests to another, even for payment, he demonstrates great trust. His virtue is greater.'

'You're sure?' the corpse-spirit hissed, but it did not wait for an answer. It was gone, and the king had to again return to collect it.

STORY 9

Vows

Another story began, and just as the journeys to and from the charnel ground never changed, this story seemed to echo others the king had heard before.

Ah sire, once there was a city called Madanapuram, famed for its ancient crimson temple dedicated to Mahādevī. During the reign of King Madanavira the Compassionate, it was the home of a merchant, Hiranyadatta, and his daughter, Madanasenā, a girl in the radiant first bloom of womanhood. One spring afternoon, she was wandering in her father's garden with her friends. The marriage her father had arranged for her long ago was soon to take place, and, though she had never set eyes on her prospective husband, her friends and she were bursting with excitement.

The same afternoon, Somadatta, another merchant's son, wandering with his male friends in nearby woods, strayed into Hiranyadatta's garden. There, they encountered a laughing crowd of girls. When Somadatta and Madanasenā saw each other, they saw no one else in the world. Yearning, like a forest fire, swept them up, body and soul. He reached out and seized her hand. She did not resist. 'You have set my heart on fire. I will die if you do not love me,' he blurted.

The girl protested: 'You must not say such a thing. To kill yourself is a sin.'

But he couldn't stop: 'Love is destroying me. That our bodies are separated, even by an inch, causes me physical pain. This pain is burning my heart and mind to ash. I no longer care about right or wrong. Only if you promise to meet me will my soul remain in my body.' He held her hand tightly, and she trembled as the heat of his body and the passion of his words ignited the flames of desire in her.

'Oh,' she cried, 'I have never craved anyone as I crave you. But in five days, I must marry a man my father chose for me when I was a child, a man I've never seen.'

Somadatta burst in, 'I don't care. Married. Not married. Fate has brought us together. We are destined to be lovers.'

'It must be,' Madanasenā agreed. 'It must.'

But the sun was beginning to set. The two would soon have to part. 'Somadatta is my name,' he said and he told her his father's name and where he lived.

'I am Madanasenā,' she answered, 'and I will let you know when can meet.' If their friends had not been nearby, they would have embraced.

Five days later, Madanasenā was married to a handsome and wealthy man who took her to his home. She had her own apartment in her new house; she shut the door and refused to leave. After a few days, her three sisters-in-law burst in, took hold of her, dressed her in beautiful robes and jewels and forced her into her husband's bedroom. Head down, she sat silently in the corner, arms, hands covering her face. Her husband took her hands, lifted her gently and led her to the bed. He was about to put his arms around her when she pushed him away. She told him that she had promised her love to Somadatta. The husband pulled away. 'If that is truly your desire, then follow it,' he said with a shrug of resignation. Madanasenā rushed out the door and through dark streets to the merchant's house.

Now it happened that a thief was prowling the streets that night, and when he saw a young woman wearing silk robes, adorned with jewelled necklaces, bracelets and earrings, hurrying through the shadows, he could not believe his luck. She shrank back as he came up to her, smiling. 'Young lady, tell me this. Why is such a young and beautiful girl, wearing such valuable robes and a fortune in jewels, wandering alone in the streets at midnight?'

The young woman replied boldly: 'I am going to the arms of the man I adore.'

'And who will protect you on this journey?'

'Kāmadeva, the God of Passion and Love, protects me with his bow and arrow, even now.' Then she told the thief everything and ended: 'Sir, I beg you, do not rip my clothes and steal my jewels. Let my lover see me adorned this way. When I leave his bed, I promise you may take everything.'

The thief was not a heartless man. He agreed to wait by the door of the mansion while the girl met her lover. Madanasenā found Somadatta deep asleep. She shook him and began kissing him. He did not know if he was dreaming or awake. 'Are you the divine daughter of a god, the offspring of a sage or a Nāga princess risen from the sea?' he asked. 'Who are you and why are you here?'

She replied: 'I am Madanasenā, the daughter of the merchant, Hiranyadatta. Five days ago in my father's garden, you held my hand and swore your love to me. I had never felt such passion. Though I was about to be married, I promised to come to you. Now, even before I slept with my husband, I am here.'

Somadatta was incredulous and asked: 'You told your husband?'

Madasenā laughed. 'I did. And he told me to come to you.'

Somadatta stood up, pulled on his robe and chided her as he paced: 'It is said that dirty clothes diminish whoever wears them; bad food weakens whoever eats it; a bad son ruins his family; a wicked wife destroys a husband. Demons cannot help killing; a woman can only cause trouble.' He shook his head. 'Even so, a woman is the most magical, the most alluring, the most radiant and transformative being in all the universe. What she does or does not do, no man will ever understand.'

He hesitated, then continued: 'No matter what I said five days ago, I cannot become involved with another man's wife.'

Somadatta turned his back and left the room. Madanasenā was shocked. She shouted after him: 'When your passion faded, you turned into a moralist. Well, at least I kept my word and told the truth.'

Tears streaming down her cheeks, the young woman ran back to the street where the thief was waiting. 'That didn't take long,' he said. She told him exactly what had happened. The thief looked at her sadly. He did not take her clothes or jewels and walked away. When Madanasenā returned to her husband, she told him everything. He looked at her coldly. He said: 'The cuckoo's beauty is found in song; the beauty of an ugly man is found in knowledge; the beauty of a devotee is found in patient suffering;

and a woman's beauty is found in fidelity to her husband. You must return to your parents.'

☠

The Vetāla then asked: 'O Wise King, of the three men in this story, whose virtue is the greatest?'

The King replied immediately: 'Obviously, the thief's.'

'And why?'

'The husband let his wife go because he could never trust such a faithless woman. The merchant's son, despite being momentarily overcome by passion, found obedience to convention preferable to passing pleasure. But the thief gained nothing from his kindness. He was a criminal but that night, his merit was greatest.'

The corpse-spirit again was gone. It was the breeze that now whispered in the treetops. There was no end to all this coming and going, and no meaning, just a cascade of fragments, all incomplete.

STORY 10

Sensitivity

'Your life, O King, must seem more and more like an illusion,' murmured the Vetāla. 'You walk back and forth like a shuttle on a loom to recover and deliver me. You hope there is a larger pattern, a larger meaning, a place in a larger story … We'll just have to see.'

The Vetāla fell silent while King Vikramāditya strode on. Then the corpse-spirit resumed.

☠

Not so long ago, the hard-working King Guneśekara ruled over the country of Gauda from his green-gated capital, Punyavardhanam. His minister, Abayaćandra, was an ardent adherent of the Jain religion and sought to persuade the king to follow that path.

The minister said to the king: 'Great sire, to enact good laws, you must understand cause and effect. Birth and death are inseparable for anyone in any world. Pangs of love or anger, or covetousness or neglect, propel us into one existence after another. We are born over and over and we die again and again. Unceasingly, we move from realm to realm carried on by the confusions of birth and the pains of sickness and death. Even the Gods are not spared.

'To escape the endless cycles of rebirth, we must never harm others: we must always be kind. A cow is superior to a god because she is content, free from the five conflicting emotions, and her milk satisfies the needs of others. The sons of cows pull carts and carriages, carry endless burdens and are cherished because they do all they can to ease the hardships of humanity. They are sacred and more worthy of worship than the deities. It is obviously then our duty to protect the lives of all animals, from ants to elephants, including fish, birds, serpents, worms, butterflies and human beings. There is no better way to escape the infinite cycle of birth and death. There is no higher duty in this world.

'But those who sustain their bodies by eating the flesh of other living beings will suffer the torments of hell. Those who live by ending the life of others will themselves be killed. Whatever part of another living being they eat will be damaged in their next life. Drinking liquor is also a sin: it causes selfish ignorance, uncontrolled desires, immersion in sense-pleasures and delirium. These states lead disastrous acts and innumerable crimes. Thus, eating meat and drinking liquor are great sins. Since it is our highest duty to preserve life, all human beings must abstain from these things.'

With these words, the minister succeeded in converting the king to the Jain faith. Whatever he advised, the king did. He no longer respected any Brahmin, ascetic, wandering yogi or religious mendicant. He governed his kingdom according to Jain teachings. In his kingdom, it was forbidden to worship Śiva or Viśnu, make offerings to Mahādevī, sacrifice cattle, donate land to temples, make offerings to the dead or leave their bodies in the Ganges. It was forbidden to gamble, drink alcohol or swim naked. With the king's ardent approval, the minister proclaimed that whoever did these things would be beaten, expelled from their homes or have their property confiscated.

Thus, King Guneśekara ruled over his kingdom until one day he fell beneath the heel of the Lord of Death. Jain laws may have benefitted the late king's subjects in their subsequent existences, but such rigour did not please them in this life. The king's son, Dharmadvaja, disagreed with the strict path his father had imposed. The new king, his friends and supporters wanted to eat meat and drink liquor; he rescinded all his father's puritanical laws. The minister Abayaćandra was seized, the hair on his head twisted into seven braids and his face blackened with tar. Tied facing backwards on a donkey, he was paraded through the streets to the sounds of fifes and drums. The populace, delighted to resume their sinful pleasures, turned out clapping and jeering. Abayaćandra was sent into exile, leaving the new king free to govern without worrying about the cosmic implications of his decisions.

Thirty years passed. One gentle summer evening, Dharmadvaja and his three wives strolled in the palace garden around a tiled pool filled with lotuses in full bloom. Impulsively, the king stripped off his clothes and dove into the water. He plucked a lotus blossom and swam over to give it to his first queen. As he handed it to her, it slipped from his hand and struck her foot. She screamed. As if the blossom had become solid iron, it broke the bones in her foot. The king leapt from the pool, called for his doctors and cradled her foot to ease her pain. Night fell, and a ruby-red full moon rose in the black sky. Moonbeams the colour of blood fell on the second queen's face and arms. Blisters broke out wherever they touched her. She moaned in agony. At the same time, just as dinner was to be served, the court harpist came to play languid love songs. When she heard the first plangent notes, the third queen experienced such piercing agony that she fainted and fell to the ground.

The Vetāla paused and, instead of resuming the story, he asked the king, 'Sire, which of these excellent women do you think was the most sensitive?'

King Vikramāditya was surprised to be questioned before the story reached a conclusion. 'Oh, without doubt, it was the third queen,' he replied. 'The very sensations that had once brought the queens such pleasure now caused them excruciating pain. But the first and second both succumbed when something touched them. The third queen responded only to a distant sound. Obviously then, she is the most sensitive.' The king was trying to formulate a question about this, but the Vetāla was gone.

The king was again cutting him down from a tree, throwing him over his shoulder like an empty sack, and continuing his journey.

STORY 11

Love and Ruling

The corpse-spirit whispered: 'I hope you find this story more satisfactory.'

Once, there was a city called Gunapura where all the buildings were white as chalk. King Jannavallabha, notoriously self-indulgent, ruled here, and Prajnakośa was his minister. One hot day, the king said to his minister: 'Is any pleasure in this world more intense than sexual pleasure?'

'No,' the minister replied.

'Well then,' the king considered, 'why should I forego the pleasures of sex even for a moment merely to rule a kingdom?'

And with that, he renounced his responsibilities so that he could devote all his days and nights to erotic delight. Gorgeous and seductive women, large or small, dark or fair, voluptuous or willowy, experienced or innocent, cultured or ignorant, were brought to him from all around the world. He immersed himself in every kind of amorous bliss, leaving the cares of ruling to his minister.

Overseeing the continuous needs of state and catering to the endless desires of his sovereign exhausted Prajnakośa.

Disconsolately, he stared out his bedroom window down at the garden below. His wife said: 'Fatigue is undermining your health.'

He replied, 'Truly, my strength is declining while the king is swimming in bliss.'

The minister's wife then said: 'You have worked loyally and without cease. The king is happy; the kingdom is prosperous and at peace. Tell the king you wish to go on a pilgrimage.'

The minister was silent. Later, however, he went to the king who gave his permission.

Prajnakośa set off dressed as a humble pilgrim. Within a few days, he reached Rāmeśvaram, the holy beach where, at Lord Rāma's command, Hanumān once built a bridge to Sri Lanka. There, the minister came across a lustrous pink marble temple devoted to the Great Goddess Mahādevī. He entered the shade of its vaulted interior and gave praises and offerings to the deity. Returning outside, he gazed across the shimmering sea. Gradually from beneath the pale blue waves rose a huge golden tree with leaves of emeralds, blossoms of topaz and fruits of coral. Its dazzling beauty was almost blinding. The pervasive scent of lotus flowers was entrancing. Sitting amid the emerald leaves and golden branches was a young woman of radiant loveliness. She held a lute of pearl and sang music unlike any he had ever heard. He was enraptured by her voice and the haunting melancholy of the melodies she sang. He didn't know how long he stood there until slowly the tree and the young woman dissolved back into the sea.

Prajnakośa returned to Gunapura as quickly as he could. He went to the king, prostrated himself and held his hands together as he spoke. 'Your Majesty, I have seen a marvel unlike anything I could imagine.'

'Tell me,' said the king.

'O Great Sovereign,' the minister continued, 'wise men of long ago maintained we should not speak of things we do not understand. I do not comprehend what I just saw, heard, even smelled. But I did experience something inexplicable, and since this is so, I will tell you.'

The king stirred impatiently, and the minister recounted what he had experienced as clearly as he could. 'I was speechless,' he concluded. 'I could not move, but as soon as I had recovered, I came back to tell you of this marvel.'

The king did not hesitate. Leaving Prajnakośa to govern, he took his swiftest horse and rode to the seashore.

Arriving at Rāmeśvaram, the king entered the temple and worshipped the All-Embracing One with prayers and offerings. He emerged to gaze at the shining blue-green waves, and soon, exactly as his minister had described, a golden tree rose from the sea, glittering with many-coloured jewels and filling the air with an irresistible perfume. He was transported. The woman who sat singing with such sorrow in the gold branches was more beautiful than desire itself. The king dove into the sea, climbed up the branches and sat beside her. The tree sank into the waves and carried the king and the woman down into the realm of the Nāgas, semi-serpent beings of great splendour and wealth, who dwell beneath the oceans, lakes and rivers of the world. They are renowned for their subtlety and courage; their daughters are more enchanting than any earthly women.

'O most valiant of men,' the Nāga princess said. 'Who are you and why are you here?'

'I am Jannavallabha, king of Gunapura,' the king replied. 'Your unworldly beauty completely overpowered me.'

The princess smiled and took his hand. 'I am Sundari, daughter of the Nāga lord, Vidyādhara,' she declared. 'I will marry you right now, but you must promise to abstain from having sex with me until after the fourteenth night of the waning moon.'

The king gave his word and thus the two were married. On the fourteenth night after their marriage, the princess said to the king: 'Tonight, when darkness falls and the waters turn black, you must not stay near me. Go away and wait.'

Again, the king gave his word, and yet he could not bear to leave her out of his sight. He unsheathed his sword, hid nearby and kept watch over her. At midnight, a huge, shiny black demon, covered with pale seaweed, with red fangs and three yellow eyes, came and snatched the princess in its arms. The king was afraid, but he saw his wife struggling to escape. The demon leered vacantly as it embraced her. The king leapt to attack, screaming at the top of his lungs. He swung his sword and cut through the demon's neck. Its head fell slowly to the ocean floor. Greenish blood streamed from the demon's neck, until finally it lay dead. 'O Noble King, you have freed me!' Sundarī sobbed and went on: 'My Lord, it is not every mountain that contains rubies. Not every forest has sandalwood trees. Not every elephant has ivory tusks. It is not every city that contains a true man. You are a jewel in a world of stones.'

The king then asked: 'What kind of curse compelled you, on the fourteenth night of the waning moon, to meet with this creature?'

The princess was embarrassed. 'Since I was a child, my father could not bear to eat his dinner unless I attended him. This is how things were. One day, I don't remember why, I could not be with him. My father is intemperate. Enraged, he shouted: "You must learn to keep appointments." And he pronounced a dreadful curse on me: "On the fourteenth night of the waning moon, a creature of supreme ugliness will come and embrace you. You must remain a virgin and keep this tryst secret or you will live all your life alone." Almost instantly, he regretted saying this, but words once spoken cannot be taken back. "Father," I cried. "Can this curse ever end?" He said: "When a brave king comes and kills the demon, you will be free." Now you have delivered me. I owe you my life. Let us receive my father's blessing.'

King Jannavallabha was reluctant to meet such an unpredictable and powerful being. He said: 'Let us go to my kingdom now. We can visit your father later.'

The princess agreed, and when the two arrived in Gunapura, the news of the king's beautiful bride spread through the city. Citizens lined the street; there was feasting and music in every house. Wealthy citizens came to the court to offer congratulations. The king gave lavishly to Brahmins, yogis, mendicants and the poor. Together the couple enjoyed every pleasure and sated every lust. Sometimes, other consorts joined them. Each day, their desires were as keen as the first, and each moment of bliss was more intense than the last. The king left all responsibility of governing to his faithful minister.

Some months later, the king asked his bride: 'Should we not, as I promised, visit your father?'

The princess replied: 'We need not go.'

When the king then asked her why, she confessed: 'O King, my father is a Nāga, a demigod. My intimacies with you have made me yours. I am no longer what I was. My father would have no more respect for me. I am now more human than Nāga. He would barely recognize me.'

How the princess felt about this the king could not tell, but he was utterly overjoyed. He celebrated, giving lavishly to all the people in his kingdom.

When Prajnakośa heard what was happening, he died of a broken heart on the spot.

The story was over. The forest was silent.

'O Great King,' asked the corpse-spirit, 'why did the minister die?'

It took King Vikramāditya only a moment to answer. 'The minister saw that the king would never rule his kingdom, nor would he take responsibility for his people. Eventually, his sensual obsessions would deplete the country. The minister knew that to obey the king would lead to the end of his dynasty. He found this unendurable, and he died.'

The Vetāla again was gone. Again, King Vikramāditya set off after him. The forest had little scent. Everything seemed somehow pale, lifeless and would remain so, thought the king, until the demon began another tale.

STORY 12

Uncaused

King Vikramāditya walked back and forth in the dank empty forest, losing the Vetāla, collecting it, losing it again, carrying it again. He was in a dream from which he could not wake. And within that dream, he entered and left other story-dreams that engulfed him, seemed real and then disappeared without having changed anything. The corpse-demon's stories, which he offered as distractions, had become the most real part of the king's journey. And so, from the cold misty presence on his shoulder, a whisper emerged and another story began.

Devasvāmi was the royal guru of King Ćudāmini, an irritable man. He dwelt in Ćudāpura, a city with four pale turquoise spires. The guru's son, Harisvāmi, was as beautiful as Kāmadeva, God of Desire, as learned in science and spiritual matters as Brhaspati, Tutor of the Gods, and accumulated riches as easily as Kubera, God of Wealth. He married a Brahmin's daughter, Lavanyavati, who was beautiful and wise enough to be worthy of him. Their love for each other filled every moment of their lives.

One hot summer night, they were deep asleep on the roof of their summer pavilion. A cool breeze rose, and Lavanyavati's veil slipped from her face. At that very moment, an air deity, a Vidyādhara, was riding his gilded chariot in the night sky and happened to see her. He was instantly captivated by her gentle beauty. He descended, lifted her into his carriage and rose into the darkness between the stars. Lavanyavati believed she was dreaming and did not stir.

In the cool of early morning, Harisvāmi awoke. He reached out to caress his wife, but leaving only for a wisp of her scent, she had vanished. He called to her, but she did not answer. Alarmed, he ran down the stairs to search the house. When he did not find her, he called his servants and together they combed the streets, the neighbourhood and the whole city. 'Who has stolen her?' he wailed. 'Where can she be?'

Desperately, Harisvāmi returned home and searched the house a second time, then a third and fourth and a fifth. He lost all hope. As days and weeks went by, he found the house ever more desolate. Everything that formerly gave him pleasure now mocked him. Day and night, he wept and cried out: 'O Love, O Heart, O Life of my Soul.' His life lost all meaning, and finally he renounced the world. Having given away his house and possessions, he wrapped a loincloth around his waist, rubbed ashes of burnt cow dung on his body, put a rosary of bone around his neck and left the city to wander the world as a beggar. He walked through forests and across plains, from town to village to city without stopping anywhere for long.

One day at noon, he entered a small village. He was starving. He went to a Brahmin's house and, holding out his bowl, begged for food. His vanished wife still obsessed him: he was indifferent to what he ate. The Brahmin took the bowl into his house and brought it back, heaped with rice boiled in milk. Harisvāmi went to wash at a nearby pool and put the food on the pool's tiled edge. From the roots of a nearby tree, a small venomous black snake slithered out, sank its fangs into the rice and filled it with poison. Harisvāmi began eating and after only one bite, he felt poison burning through his system. He staggered to the Brahmin's house and cried out: 'Why have you poisoned me?' He collapsed and died. Shocked to see the beggar dead at his gate, the Brahmin ran into the kitchen and screamed at his wife: 'You killed a holy man. My family is cursed. You must leave us.'

The Vetāla stopped. 'O Wise King, in this world, every action has a consequence, and there is no effect without a cause. Thus, my question is this: "Who is responsible for killing Harisvāmi?"'

King Vikramāditya answered immediately: 'The snake is naturally poisonous, so it is blameless. The Brahmin did a kindness in giving food to a starving man. He is not guilty of anything but generosity. The Brahmin's wife did what her husband asked. She too is guiltless. Harisvāmi ate the milk and rice without any suspicion of poison. Therefore, he too is innocent.'

The corpse-demon pressed: 'So there are evil deeds without a cause?'

'Well,' replied the king, 'the deed had a cause, but not the evil.'

But then the Vetāla emitted a cold little laugh. 'O King, is it wise for a ruler to admit that good and evil may be outside his judgement?'

Again the Vetāla vanished, the king walked, the corpse was swinging from the tree, the king was cutting him down, carrying him, listening, and everything was beginning all over again.

STORY 13

Love and Chaos

The king was tired and the world felt remote. Almost confidingly, the corpse-spirit whispered, 'Sire, I must tell another story. Like you, I cannot stop. You know we the dead live only as tales are told.' With a faint rattle like dry leaves in a breeze, the Vetāla cleared its throat.

Once, O Peerless Majesty, the proud King Ranadhīra ruled Ćandradarśanam, a city always covered in yellow dust. In this city lived Dharmadhvaja, a prosperous merchant, with his daughter, Ksobini, a young woman of surpassing allure. At that time, a band of robbers plagued Ćandradarśanam. Every merchant had been robbed at least once, most more, and all were outraged. Together, they confronted the king. 'Your Majesty, we mean no disrespect, but thieves infest your city like moths in a clothes closet. Every day our wealth is stolen from our homes and trade goods are taken from our warehouses. Soon we will have no business at all. But before that happens, sire, we will leave and go someplace where we can prosper.'

King Ranadhīra nodded. 'I understand. I will take care of it.'

The king brought in guards and mercenaries to patrol the streets and keep watch over the merchants' possessions. He ordered them to kill every thief they found.

Day and night, armed guards patrolled the city, but soon the robberies resumed. Again, the merchants came to the king. 'Sire, you have indeed sent guards, but in vain. Like locusts, thieves still devour our goods.'

King Ranadhira replied, 'From tonight on, I myself will guard the city.' He put on his armour and, bearing his sword and shield, he went out into his city alone and on foot. Late that night, he saw someone slinking towards him. 'Who are you?' the king shouted.

The man replied with a laugh, 'A thief. And you?'

'I too am a thief,' said the king.

'Well,' the thief suggested, 'let's do some thieving together.'

They went to a prosperous part of the city, where they broke into two locked mansions and stole jewellery, gold coins and silver tableware. The thief led the way as they carried their loot to a well outside the city. Inside the well, a stone staircase curved down deep into the underworld, and it took the men ten minutes to reach the bottom.

'This is my home,' the thief told the king as they passed through a vast cavern lined with cave dwellings. 'Wait here while I give our plunder to the Demon Lord of Thieves.' But while he waited, a servant hired from the world above recognized King Ranadhīra. 'What are you doing here? Your Majesty, this is an evil place. Leave or the demon will kill you. Let me guide you.' And so, the king was able to return safely to his palace.

The next day, the king gathered his guards and soldiers and invaded the underworld. Placing his best and bravest soldiers at the front of his forces, the king led his men down the staircase in the well. The Demon Lord of Thieves heard them coming. So, when King Ranadhīra and the vanguard of his army entered the underworld cavern, the Demon Lord's green phosphorescent body had swelled to an enormous size; its teeth were axe blades, its hair were razors and its iron claws swords. Spitting molten iron and roaring like an avalanche, it burned, cut, slaughtered and devoured the king's men. None could withstand its lethal power. The king turned and ran. He reached the foot of the staircase when his thief-companion from the night before appeared from the shadows, brandishing a sabre and shouting: 'Are you afraid to meet my Demon Lord?'

The king drew his sword. The two fought until the thief was faint from many wounds. The king dragged him by the hair up the stairs, determined to have at least one captive.

Back in his palace, King Ranadhīra had his doctors attend to the thief and put him in prison. He summoned all the merchants, traders and businessmen and addressed them: 'Just outside our city is an abandoned well and staircase. It is a portal to a demon realm and the source of all the crime that afflicts us. The demon is too powerful to kill and those he seduces too numerous. But by blocking up the well with rocks and rubble, we can end the lawlessness and chaos. This must be done immediately.' None who did business in the city hesitated; all sent their workers to collect boulders and stones to fill the well. By nightfall, the portal was completely barricaded.

The next day, the king had the thief washed, dressed in silk robes, tied, seated backwards on a camel and paraded through the city. A crier walked next to him, beating a drum and shouting:

'King Ranadhīra captured this thief who held our city hostage. Tomorrow he will be impaled in front of Mahādevī's temple.'

As the grisly parade passed by the merchant Dharmadhvaja's house, his daughter Ksobini asked her maid: 'What is this racket? Have they caught the thief?'

'Yes, mistress,' her maid replied. 'He is so handsome. Come see. He's going to be impaled.'

Ksobini ran to the window. One glance and she was enslaved by the thief's insolent appeal. She ran to her father and implored: 'Go to the king. You must stop the execution. Bring the thief home. I want him.'

Her father was shocked. 'Why?' he asked. 'Why would the king release this murderous thief?'

Mad with lust, Ksobini berated her father. 'Offer him everything. I love him. If I don't marry him, I will kill myself.'

The merchant went to the king. 'O Merciful One,' he begged, 'take all I own but set this thief free.'

The king was astonished. 'How can you ask such a thing? This is a man who robbed you and all the others here. It was you who wanted me to kill him. It was because of him that a demon devoured my army. He shall not live.'

The merchant returned home and told his daughter that despite his offer, the king was resolved that the thief would die.

By now, the thief had been brought to the execution grounds. A freshly sharpened post on which to impale him had been set in the ground in front of the Great Goddess's temple. All around, people were gossiping about the merchant and how his daughter had fallen in love with the condemned thief. When the thief heard this, he laughed aloud, then wept bitterly. He was taken off the camel and placed atop the post; the crowd pulled him down by his legs and arms until he was impaled through the chest and he died.

When word of the thief's death reached the merchant's daughter, she decided she had to follow him in death. She had a funeral pyre built on the execution ground next to the post where the thief's body was still impaled. She mounted the pyre and ordered that the body of this man she loved be brought to her. With his head in her lap, she signalled her servants to light the pyre and sat quietly waiting for the flames to engulf her. But as the flames rose, the temple door opened and there stood the Goddess herself, black and shining, her hair swirling like smoke and lips the colour of fire. The flames stopped. 'Daughter,' she called in a gentle voice, 'your devotion, your determination to die for love, fills me with joy. Whatever you ask for, I will grant.'

'O Mother of My Soul, restore this man to life.'

'It shall be so.'

In the blink of an eye, the thief was again alive.

Then the corpse-spirit, in his familiar confiding voice, said, 'So, Great King, tell me: why, on learning his fate, did the thief first laugh and then cry?'

The king hesitated for a second and thought his head would split. 'I know both.' As he spoke, the pain disappeared. 'O Vetāla, when the thief heard that the merchant's daughter loved him, he thought: "Fate is perverse. A fool inherits vast wealth. A genius is born a slave. A blind man inherits a library. Just so, a woman beautiful, young and rich falls in love with me on the day I am to die." So he laughed. Then he thought: "She would give up everything for me, but I have nothing to give her." And so he wept.'

While his last word still in the air, the king found himself again alone, walking through the night.

STORY 14

Illusions

'Listen, O Great One,' the Vetāla began again in his silky voice.

Once there was a city of great wealth called Kusumavati, with roofs of red tile. The king Suvićāra was known for his compassion. His daughter, Ćandraprabha, had just blossomed into womanhood and was, indeed, beautiful.

Adjoining the king's palace were elaborate gardens, open to the public except when the royal family visited. One spring afternoon, Ćandraprabha and her ladies-in-waiting were strolling in the garden amidst its flowerbeds and fountains, telling stories and laughing. A handsome young Brahmin named Vāmanasvami was sleeping in the shade of a banyan tree. He had not heard the gates close, but the voices of the women, chattering and giggling, woke him with a start. The princess was staring down at him, her eyebrows arched in astonishment. Like water poured into water, their gazes mingled and they were lost to all the world. Kāma, the God of Desire, held them in his power. Vāmanasvami fainted and lay unmoving as if dead. Princess Ćandraprabha staggered and her whole body shook. She could not speak. Her attendants reached out to keep her from falling. They called for a litter and carried her back into the palace. The Brahmin's son lay on the ground, unconscious. Even the next morning, he remained unaware as servants reopened the park and visitors wandered in.

Among those now walking in the royal garden were two men from Knavru, Śaśi and Mūladeva. Disguised as Brahmins, they were swindlers skilled in magic, medicine and the occult. Mūladeva noticed the handsome young man lying motionless beneath a tree. 'Śaśi, is that man dead?' he asked. The two men took a closer look.

Śaśi said: 'No, he has merely lost his senses Perhaps the arrows of love have pierced his heart.'

'Let's wake him up,' said Mūladeva.

'Why bother?' Śaśi replied. But Mūladeva was already sprinkling water from a nearby fountain on the handsome young man. Vāmanasvami stirred and rubbed his eyes. 'Is anything wrong, young sir?' Mūladeva asked.

Vāmanasvami immediately was suspicious. 'I was taught to share my troubles only with those who can help me.'

Mūladeva laughed. 'Excellent advice no doubt, but my friend and I devise remedies for troubles of all kinds. You can trust us.' The man had an honest face and sounded sincere, so Vāmanasvami believed him. 'Just now, I saw Princess Ćandraprabha walking through the garden with her ladies in waiting,' he confided. 'I was overwhelmed by her beauty; our eyes met, and I fainted. If we cannot marry, I will die.'

Then Mūladeva said: 'Come with us. We can obtain the princess for you. If we fail, we give our word as Brahmins that we will repay you. You have nothing to lose.'

Vāmanasvami was enraged. 'A woman is more valuable than wealth of any kind. If I cannot have the woman who has captivated me, what is the point of wealth? I would rather be a wretched beast than live without the princess.'

'It will be as you desire,' Mūladeva said. 'I give my word: Princess Ćandraprabha shall be yours.'

The three went to Mūladeva's and Śaśi's residence where Mūladeva set to work making two magic pills. When he was done, he gave one to Vāmanasvami. 'When you put this pill in your mouth, you will be transformed into a beautiful fourteen-year-old girl. When you remove it from your mouth, you will again be as you are now. Don't swallow the pill. Now, put it in your mouth.' Vāmanasvami did so and at once he turned into a lovely young girl. Then Mūladeva put the other pill in his own mouth. Immediately he became an eighty-year-old Brahmin. He and the girl went off to the palace to see the king.

When the distinguished and aged Brahmin entered the throne room with a shy and beautiful young woman holding his hand, the king had chairs set out for them. Before he sat, the Brahmin chanted a blessing: 'May you whose glory pervades the three worlds surpass all other worldly rulers; may you who lifts mountains in his hand to shelter his devotees from Indra's thunderbolts be forever indestructible; may Viśnu himself in all his myriad forms and avatars ever care for you and protect you.' With a low bow, the Brahmin and the young girl sat.

The king was moved and asked: 'Where, O Worthy One, have you come from, and what brings you here?'

And Mūladeva, in his guise as the aged Brahmin, replied: 'O Great King, I come from the far side of the Ganges where I and my family lived for centuries. Recently, our homeland was overrun by rebel soldiers who were no more than thieves. People scattered in all directions to escape. In the chaos, my wife and son disappeared, but I found my son's wife, lost in the forest. I have brought her to your safe and prosperous domain, hoping that Your Majesty will take care of her while I continue to search for my wife and son. She is too delicate and fearful to accompany me. Sire, please look after her as if she were your own.'

The king was sympathetic but reluctant and thought: 'What can I do? This Brahmin has great powers. If I do not take her in, he may curse me and my kingdom.'

So he replied: 'O wise one, set your mind at ease. I will honour your wish.'

Then he called for Princess Ćandraprabha. The Princess had of late seemed distraught; she was pale and drawn. Perhaps a companion would do her good. 'My dearest child,' he said. 'Take this young woman to your quarters. Take care of her day and night, waking or sleeping or moving about. Give her anything she wants. Make sure she is content and do not let her out of your sight for even a moment.'

The Brahmin bowed and expressed his deepest thanks. Promising to return when he had found his family, he departed. The princess led the Brahmin's daughter-in-law by the hand to her own quarters. That night, sleeping in the same bed, they began to talk. The young girl asked: 'How can it be that one so young and so beautiful now looks so downcast and sickly?'

Whispering in the darkness, the princess explained: 'Not long ago, my ladies-in-waiting and I went walking in the royal gardens. Sleeping under a banyan tree, I saw a handsome young Brahmin, as beautiful as the God of Desire. I gazed at him just as he opened his eyes and he gazed back until we both fainted.

Now, every second of every day, I think of him and dream of him throughout the night. I imagine him near me. I only want him. I cannot eat or drink. I am wasting away.'

When the girl heard this, she asked: 'What will you give me if I bring him into your arms?'

The princess burst out: 'I will be your slave forever.'

With a smile, the girl took the pill from her mouth. Suddenly, she was the young Brahmin who had so ignited the princess's passion. The princess did not know if she was awake or dreaming; she blushed. Overcome with desire, Vāmanasvami was back in his own form. Like twigs in a fire, the two twined together, joined without ceremony or permission in marriage. Vāmanasvami went back to taking the young woman's form by day and his own by night. Their desire was insatiable. At the end of six months, the princess was pregnant.

Around then, the king and his family happened to attend the wedding of his minister's daughter. Vāmanasvami, as a girl, joined in the celebrations. When the minister's reckless, pampered son saw her, he fell in love. He had one wife but now desired this girl as a second. He was desperate and said to his friend: 'If I cannot have that girl, I will kill myself.'

Not long after, the king and his family returned to his palace. None suspected what the minister's son intended. A month passed; the minister's son stopped eating or drinking. His friend could not bear to see such misery and told the minister about his son's great new love. The minister went to the king, prostrated himself and asked: 'Most Generous of Sovereigns, my son has fallen in love with the aged Brahmin's daughter-in-law, whom you care for as your own. He will neither eat nor drink. I beg you: give this girl to my son or he will die.'

The king refused. 'I have sworn to the Brahmin that I would take care of her. A king cannot break his word.'

The minister returned home in despair. He could not bear seeing his son in misery; he too then lost his appetite for food and drink and began to waste away. Seeing his precipitous decline, the officials who served him went to the king. The eldest spoke first. 'O Wise King, the minister is grieving because his son is suffering for love. If he dies, sire, who will administer the affairs of state? The kingdom will fall into ruin. Would it not be better to allow his son to marry the Brahmin's daughter-in-law?'

The king asked other officials for their opinion; all agreed: 'Majesty, it is many months since the old Brahmin left here. Neither the gods of earth or sky can say whether he is alive or dead. It is both reasonable and right for you to give that Brahmin's daughter to the minister's son, especially if this will preserve the well-being of your kingdom. Should the Brahmin return, give him gold and land. Find another wife for his son if he too is still alive. There is no fault in such generous deeds.'

The king was persuaded. He sent for the girl and told her: 'Your father-in-law left you here as my ward. My minister's son has, however, fallen under your spell; he wants you to become his second wife. I have agreed to this.'

The girl, Vāmanasvami in disguise, burst out: 'Indeed, it is true: a merchant's wealth vanishes when no one guards it; a Brahmin's virtue is lost when he serves a king; and a woman's virtue is destroyed when she is considered beautiful.'

Weeping, she continued, 'Your Majesty has given me all I could wish for and I must obey you. But, if I am to be this man's wife, you must command this minister's son to grant my request.'

'And what is that?' the king asked.

His ward replied: 'I am of the Brahmin caste. The minister's son is of the Kśatriya caste. We all must live according to the order into which we are born. He must make himself acceptable to my ancestors by performing pilgrimages to all the sacred Brahmin sites. Only then can I marry him.'

The king agreed and told the minister's son: 'Only if you visit and pay homage at all the sacred Brahmin places, will I give this girl to you.'

The minister's son replied: 'Since she has agreed to be my wife, she should live in my house.'

The young woman saw no way to object. When she came to her future husband's house, he introduced her to his first wife, saying: 'You do not know each other, and I will be gone for some time, but you must live together peacefully. Do not quarrel and fight. Be affectionate to one another and do not visit strangers.' He then left on his pilgrimage.

The two wives found they had much in common, not least of which was their lack of affection for the minister's son. Often, they lay side by side and chatted. Late one warm night, the first wife, Saubhagyasundari by name, confided that her husband left her desires unfulfilled. 'I am on fire,' she said. 'But will I ever know the bliss such yearning promises?'

The other replied: 'What will you give me if I satisfy your passion?'

'I will be your slave,' Saubhagyasundari said. The Brahmin's daughter-in-law took the pill from her mouth, and the beautiful and virile Vāmanasvami now stood before her. That night and for all the nights following, they made love until dawn. They passed their days together and fell ever more deeply in love.

Six months later, the minister's son returned from his pilgrimage. His household, friends and neighbours came to greet him; his father's assistants, attendants and slaves thronged the streets to celebrate.

Taking the pill from his mouth, Vāmanasvami snuck out through the back gate. He sought out Mūladeva and Śaśi and told them about the adventures their pill made possible. He described the pleasures of being a woman. The three laughed that their deceptions had been so successful and decided to take their ruse still further. A pill returned Mūladeva to his form as the imposing old Brahmin, and Śaśi's pill turned him into a strong young Brahmin who could pose as the old man's long-lost son. They went to the palace to see the king and Vāmanasvami, again a woman, returned home.

The king greeted the Brahmin and his son warmly and put them at ease. After they chanted blessings for the king and his domain, the king asked the old Brahmin: 'What kept you away so long?'

'O Most Powerful King, for months, I searched for my wife and my son. I found my wife was dead and performed her funeral. After many more months, it was a great solace to find my son alive. Now, thanks to your kindness, he and his beloved wife will at last be reunited. We will finally return to our homeland as a family.'

The king was sick with regret and shame. He had no choice but to explain what he had done with the young man's wife. The old Brahmin burst out: 'What kind of king forgets his promise? What kind of man agrees to care for another's wife, then gives her away? Well, you won't forget my curse on you.'

He was about to begin but the king interrupted, 'O Holy One, spare me.'

The Brahmin paused before replying: 'You are wise to fear the power of my words. If you wish me to let you live, you must give your daughter, Princess Ćandraprabha, in marriage to my son.' Immediately, the king agreed. Astrologers were summoned to determine the nearest auspicious time for him to have his daughter wed the old Brahmin's son. Even before the last of the celebrations were over, the two swindlers ran off, taking the princess and her enormous dowry with them.

But Vāmanasvami still loved the princess as much as when he first saw her and he followed them to their house. 'Give me back my wife!' he demanded.

Śaśi refused, saying: 'The king himself made the princess my wife.'

'That marriage was a sham,' Vāmanasvami shouted. 'She is pregnant with my child.' Their argument became more and more heated; they could find no solution.

The Vetāla stopped. The king strode on, hardly thinking. He was wondering if the corpse-demon had a question when it whispered: 'O great sire, tell me: who is the true husband of this unlucky princess? Is it the one married in a ceremony before a king and his court or is it the other, married with her body and pregnant by him?'

King Vikramāditya answered swiftly: 'No one knew she was pregnant by Vāmanasvami when she married Śaśi before the king, court and ten witnesses. Therefore, she is his wife, and her child is his child.'

'So you insist,' the Vetāla hissed, 'that an oath before king and court is truly binding, even when other factors have been of far greater consequence?'

'I do.' But the king's head was now beginning to throb.

'That's outrageous.' The Vetāla laughed in amazement.

But the king pressed on: 'The king's decision must be the last word. How else, O errant spirit, is anything stable in a world of desire, theft, cheating, ambition, madness, greed, envy, lies and delusion? Is anything really what it seems? Kings know that we live on the edge of utter chaos.'

Then, before anything seemed to change, the corpse-spirit was hanging in the tree and King Vikramāditya was cutting him down.

STORY 15

Sacrifice

King Vikramāditya had only a vague memory of cutting the rope, climbing down the tree trunk, hoisting the weightless thing onto his shoulder and setting forth again to deliver this creature, as he had promised the waiting yogi. It was only when the corpse-spirit whispered, telling another story, that the king felt he was awake.

O Great King, on Mount Gya, high in the Himalaya, dwell the Gandharvas and their consorts, the Apsarās. These celestial musicians are silver-bodied demigods; all are part-human, some are part-animal, others part-bird. Their king, at the time of this tale, was Jimutketu, whose deepest desire was to secure the well-being of his kind and harmony with the humans and others who lived amongst them.

Jimutketu's emerald palace contained a garden filled with all the plants of the world; at its centre was the Wish-Granting Tree with branches of gold, leaves of emerald, blossoms of coral and fruits of ruby. Its leaves trembled in the breeze, producing melodies of unimaginable beauty and rhythms that elicited unimaginable joy. This was the music the Gandharvas and Apsarās learned and played. One day, as King Jimutketu sat listening to the Wish-Granting Tree, the tree whispered: 'O Worthy King, you are faithful to music and please me deeply. If there is something you desire, ask it of me now.'

The king replied: 'O Source of Happiness, grant me a son so that my kingdom and my name may endure.'

'It shall be so,' the tree responded.

When soon his wife produced a son, the king was overwhelmed with delight. All the Gandharvas and Apsarās filled the skies with the music of the sun and moon and stars. The king gave lavishly to Brahmins and wandering yogis; he summoned priests to find a name for the boy. Jimut-bahan was the name they chose.

By the age of twelve, Jimut-bahan had studied all that had ever been transmitted in speaking, writing and in music. Soon he was the most accomplished of beings. His mind was compassionate, steadfast, inventive and capacious. Those his father had appointed to serve him were happy to follow his commands.

When he reached manhood, he, like his father, stayed close to the Wish-Granting Tree. Day and night, he listened to its music. The tree was pleased and whispered to the prince: 'Ask whatever you would like, and I will give it to you.'

'O Source of Joy,' Jimut-Bahan asked. 'Let all who dwell here be free from need. May all enjoy equal wealth.'

The Wish-Granting Tree made this so. Soon, everyone was wealthy, and no one needed to work for anyone else. Trade with those in other places ceased. Wealth became valueless and prosperity became indistinguishable from poverty.

Neither the king nor the prince realized that the kingdom was falling apart, so, without them knowing, all the Gandharvas and

Apsarās came together to find a way to restore some reasonable order.

'Our rulers are completely absorbed in spiritual life,' they complained. 'They have brought this kingdom to the edge of collapse. It is best to exile them and give the throne to someone more practical.'

When the Gandharvas gathered an army and surrounded the palace, the king and his son were caught completely unawares. 'What do you think we should do?' asked the king.

The prince replied, 'You know I am a master of martial arts. I can destroy them easily.'

'O Dear Son,' the king said sadly. 'Our bodies are frail. Every being, even the greatest gods, will die. It is not right to kill merely to sustain the body in its habitual condition. King Yudhiśtira won the great war in the Mahabharata only to feel everlasting regret. It is best to give up our kingdom and devote ourselves to a spiritual life.'

The prince nodded. 'It is as you say. Let us give the kingdom to our kinfolk and cultivate goodness that does not change.'

Father and son then surrendered their kingdom and ascended Mount Malaya, where they built a small retreat house for themselves. There were other retreatants not far away, and Jimut-bahan soon became friends with a sage's son living nearby. One day, when the two were out walking, they encountered a temple dedicated to Goddess Bhavāni, Giver of Life and Protector of Yogis. On entering the temple, they heard a melody of extraordinary beauty, and saw a princess, very young and alluring, lute in hand, singing a hymn to the Goddess. She looked up and her eyes met Jimut-bahan's. Love seized them both. But the princess was ashamed to have been distracted from her devotions.

She and her attendant quickly left the temple and went home. The prince was ashamed as well that the sage's son might have seen how easily his mind drifted from the path of a yogi. He too returned home. Both Jimut-bahan and the princess were filled with longing and neither could sleep that night.

At dawn, the princess and her companion returned to the temple; the prince soon followed. As the princess offered prayers and songs, the prince asked her attendant: 'This princess, what is her name? Who is her father? Is she promised to anyone?'

The companion replied: 'Her name is Malayavati. Her father is King Malayaketu. She is neither married nor betrothed. And now, my lord, could you tell me your name, your lineage and what brings you here?'

The prince told her that he was Jimut-bahan, eldest son of the king of the Gandharvas, and explained how he and his father had come to be on retreat nearby. When the princess left the temple, the prince bowed but did not follow. The princess was eager to hear what her companion had learned about the stranger.

When she learned about the prince and his father's difficulties, the princess felt a great pang of sorrow. 'How painful and sad it must be,' she thought, 'to lose your kingdom, your home, your friends.' When she returned to her father's palace, she could find neither rest nor ease. She could not stop thinking about the Gandharva prince. Day after day, he stirred constantly in her heart. Her companion saw that the princess had fallen in love. She told the queen, and the queen went to the king. 'O sire,' she said, 'it is time for our daughter to marry. Ask our son, Prince Mitravasu, to find a good husband for her.'

Prince Mitravasu spoke to the princess's companion and told the king: 'Sire, the king of the Gandharvas, Jimut-ketu, and his son, Prince Jimut-bahan, were forced to abandon their kingdom and now reside nearby. The prince is said to be handsome and accomplished; he would make a good husband for your daughter.'

The king declared: 'If this is so, I will give her to him.'

Next day, Prince Mitravasu went to the exiled king's humble lodging, introduced himself and said: 'My father, King Malayaketu, wishes your son to marry his daughter. This should be welcome to him and to you. We understand there is already a certain affection between them. And a powerful ally is good fortune for a king without a kingdom.'

The Gandharva king and his son were happy to accept the proposal. They went to King Malayaketu's castle. The prince and princess exchanged bracelets and the two kings pronounced them man and wife. They lived together in the princess's apartments in King Malayaketu's palace.

Some days later, Prince Mitravastu and Prince Jimut-bahan were taking an early morning walk on Mount Malaya. Around a bend in the path, they were astonished to see what looked like a huge pile of dried lilies, but which turned out be thousands of small, delicate white bones. 'What are these?' exclaimed Prince Jimut-bahan.

Prince Mitravasu replied: 'Above us is a cave that leads down to the realm of the Nāgas, the human-headed serpent-gods of wealth. These are the bones of young Nāgas offered each year to eagle-winged Garudas, which descend from the sky to devour them. This sacrifice allows the Nāgas to live a year in peace.'

Jimut-Bahan was deeply saddened. 'Noble Prince, would you be kind enough to leave me? I wish to pray for these unfortunate beings.' Jimut-Bahan continued alone up through a mountain ravine, and as he climbed, he heard someone weeping. Before long, he saw an aged Nāga woman with a serpent's body, sobbing. 'Why, old mother, are you weeping?' he asked, and the woman replied: 'Today, my son, Śankćur, is to be sacrificed to the Garudas.'

The prince tried to comfort her: 'This will not happen, O Aged One. I will offer myself in your son's place.'

The old Nāga's son, Śankćur, was coming down the path to bid his mother farewell and he overheard the prince. 'O noble sir,' he said, 'such compassion is rare even amongst the Gandharvas. No doubt, in the course of your life, thousands of beings will benefit from your existence; my life will benefit few. My death, however, will benefit many.'

But the prince was determined. 'I would be worthless if I didn't keep my word. Take your mother and go back where you came from.' The young Nāga and his mother did as Prince Jimutbahan insisted.

Soon, an immense Garuda descended from the sky. Its wings were wide as palace walls, its steel-sharp beak as long as a palm tree, its belly the size of a golden temple dome, its eyes as large as silver soldier's shields, and each of its feathers the size of a bronze battle spear. The Garuda swept down but the prince dodged. On the Garuda's second pass, the prince was not so lucky. The bird sliced his shoulder, catching him in its gigantic claw as it wheeled up into the sky. The prince's wedding bracelet, slick with his blood, slid off his wrist and hurtled to the ground far below. It landed in the palace garden at the princess's feet. She recognized it instantly and fainted.

After a moment, the princess recovered and ran to her parents. The bloody bracelet filled them with dread. They had no idea what could have happened; they searched in the mountains, climbing up one path, clambering down another, calling his name. The

Nāga Śankćur heard their cries, and told them of the prince's determination to sacrifice himself. They went to the place where he last saw the prince. There, the young Nāga shouted: 'O Garuda, let that man go! He is a Gandharva prince. You must not eat him! I, Śankćur, a humble Nāga, am your food!'

High above the clouds, the Garuda heard the Nāga. 'Could it be true?' he wondered. 'Could this truly be a forbidden Gandharva in my claws?'

He asked the prince: 'Who and what are you to offer up your life so easily?'

The prince replied: 'O Garuda, a tree casts shade over others while it willingly stands uncovered in the sun; likewise do trees blossom and bear fruit for the benefit of others. Trees and all noble beings share their lives with those in need. What is the use of living if one is not of use to others? Noble beings do not lose their natural qualities even if they lose their lives. Praise or blame mean nothing to them. Wealth does not remain from life to life. What does it matter if one is fat or thin? What does it matter if life is long or short? Those who walk a path of righteousness do not stray onto other paths, come what may. To cherish your own life is to live like a dog or a crow. But those who give up their lives for the sake of a Brahmin, a cow, a friend or a wife, even for the sake of a stranger, will be reborn in a celestial realm. One whose life benefits others has no regrets.'

Then the Garuda replied: 'All who live in this world cling to their lives; it is rare indeed to find someone who will sacrifice himself for another. You are an extraordinary being. I am moved by your courage. Ask me for whatever you desire. If it is within my power, I will grant it.'

Prince Jimut-bahan replied: 'O Garuda, you who penetrate the heavens, if indeed you are pleased with me, henceforth cease devouring the Nāgas and restore to life those whom you have eaten.'

The great Garuda dove through the earth as if it were nothing and drew up the water of life, which he then sprinkled on the heap of bones. Immediately their flesh returned and they came back to life. They wriggled back into the cave that led to their homeland. Then the Garuda said: 'Now, Prince Jimut-bahan, it is also my wish that your kingdom be restored to you and your father.' Saying this, the Garuda disappeared in the sky and the prince found himself with his wife, his family and Śankćur. He told them what had happened and the Nāga returned to his domain.

All who dwelt in the land of the Gandharvas also heard the news of how Prince Jimut-bahan had saved the Nāgas. Those who had taken the throne from King Jimutketu and Prince Jimut-bahan realized that these two were beings of extraordinary virtue. They felt remorse and asked them to return and take back the throne.

With that story, the corpse-demon fell silent. In a while he asked: 'O Wise King Vikramāditya, tell me this. Of all the people we encountered in this tale, whose virtue was the greatest?'

King Vikramāditya replied quickly: 'Śankćur, the young Nāga.'

'How so?' asked the Vetāla.

And Vikramāditya answered: 'Śankćur could have easily escaped but instead, he returned and offered his life to save Prince Jimut-bahan.'

'But,' asked the demon, 'the prince was willing to die for the others. Why is his virtue not at least as great if not more so?'

'The prince is of the Kśatriya caste,' the king replied. 'A warrior. He is born and raised to make such a sacrifice. This was not the case with the Nāga; his sacrifice was greater.'

Then, within seconds, as if nothing had happened in between, another story was unfolding in the dead creature's silvery voice.

STORY 16

Beauty

O Vikramāditya, King of Legend, once there was a city called Vijayapuramur, famed for its iridescent pearl-white palaces. During King Dharmaśila's reign, a wealthy merchant named Ratandatta and his only daughter, Unmādinī, resided there. When she reached womanhood, the merchant went to the king and prostrated himself: 'O Majesty, under your wise rule, I have prospered beyond imagining. It has also been my good fortune to have a daughter whose intelligence shines like the full moon and whose beauty is fresh fragrant, like a lotus newly opened. You have made all this possible, and I am deeply in your debt. I offer you my daughter, Unmādinī. Take her as your concubine or wife. If she is not to your liking, I will offer her to someone else.'

The king thanked the merchant and said that he would consider his proposal carefully.

The king summoned his three most trusted advisors and told them what the merchant proposed. 'Go and inspect this merchant's daughter,' he ordered. 'See if she is as wise and beautiful as he claims.'

The three men went to the merchant's house, and when the girl was brought out for them to examine, they were stunned. Her face shone like a full moon and her hair was dark and luminous as night. Her eyes were like a gazelle's; her nose arched nobly like a hawk's beak; her teeth were like a string of pearls; her lips were the colour of rubies. She had a waist like a leopard, a gait like a cheetah and a voice like a nightingale. Her beauty was, they agreed, a lamp blazing in a dark room. Her conversation was learned and witty and she brought everything around her to life. 'O,' the advisors said, 'her beauty would shame the goddesses in Indra's paradise.'

Smitten though they were, they were also alarmed. 'If such a woman enters the king's household, she will consume his every thought. He will be enslaved and become indifferent to governing. A multitude of disasters will consume the realm. Far better we tell him that the girl is plain as a pine board and unworthy of him.'

So they said to the king: 'The merchant's high ambitions have led him to overvalue his daughter's limited virtues. She is in no way worthy of being your consort.'

The king informed the merchant that his offer would not be accepted. Rather than waste time lamenting, the merchant gave his daughter to Balbhadra, the commanding general of the king's army.

Some months later, the king and his entourage rode past Balbhadra's residence at the very moment when Unmādinī, the general's new wife, was standing on the roof. The king happened to look up and their eyes met. His heart overflowed as her beauty filled his mind. 'Is this the daughter of a god or a Gandharva or of some demi-goddess?' he wondered. He returned to his palace in a state of agitation. 'Majesty, what has upset you so?' asked his bodyguard.

The king replied: 'While riding today, I saw a woman standing on a rooftop. My mind is like a sea in a storm.'

The bodyguard knew the route of that morning's cavalcade. 'Your Highness,' he said, 'I know the very woman you mean. She is Unmādinī, the merchant Ratandatta's daughter. The merchant had her marry your majesty's commanding general, Balbhadra.'

The king understood at once that his most trusted advisors had betrayed him. He ordered his executioner to bring the three to him immediately. Axe in hand, the executioner brought them trembling to the raging king. 'Because I trusted you, the most beautiful being on heaven or earth is now another man's wife. Can you understand my despair? Why should I not have you beheaded straightaway?"

Shaking and sweating, the advisors tried to justify themselves. 'O Merciful One, what you say is true. But we feared that from the moment you saw this extraordinary creature, you would want to only spend every minute with her. You would neglect the affairs of state and the kingdom would go to ruin. This is why we said what we did.'

The king sighed. 'Yes,' he conceded, 'what you feared would have come to pass.' He set them free but was not himself free of yearning. Day after day, he craved Unmādinī ever more intensely. He became listless and began to waste away. Soon, all the court knew the king was in love and with whom.

When General Balbhadra learnt of the king's feelings, he came to court and knelt before the king. 'O Lord of the Earth,' he said. 'I am your servant. My wife is your servant. If she can ease your suffering, she is yours.'

The king was indignant. 'What are you saying?' he snapped. 'It is wrong to take another man's wife. What kind of lawless barbarian do you think I am? As a man cherishes the feelings of his own heart, so should he cherish the feelings of others.'

But Balbadra persisted: 'My wife is mine. When I give her to you, she is yours.'

The king shook his head: 'All the world would reproach me for such a subterfuge.'

The general continued, 'Your Majesty, I shall expel her from my house. I will leave her on the street. I will leave her no choice but to become a common prostitute. Or I will have her brought to you.'

The king looked at him for a long time. 'If you do that, I will see you punished as harshly as I can.'

The king withdrew to his quarters. He could not stop thinking of Unmādinī. He could not remove her from his heart. He was unable to live without her. His longing could not be appeased. He would not eat or drink; he grew steadily weaker and within a month, he died.

When he heard this, Balbhadra was distraught and went to his guru. 'What is the proper course of action for me now?' he asked, to which the teacher replied: 'It is the servant's duty to follow his master in death.'

So, the general went to the cremation ground where the king's funeral pyre had been prepared. He bathed and made offerings and prayers. When the pyre with the king's body was set on fire, Balbhadra raised his hands to the sun and said: 'O Surya, God of the Sun, I offer my body, my every thought, my every word and my every deed so that now and in every birth to follow, I will meet with my lord King Dharmaśila and serve him through all the cycles of time.' And he leapt into the fire.

Unmādinī was overwhelmed by grief when she learned what her husband had done. She went to her teacher and asked: 'O Wise One, what now is the duty of a wife?'

Her teacher replied: 'In this world, a woman is considered to have fulfilled her destiny if she does her duty to the one to whom her parents gave her. Even if he is unworthy or a criminal, a woman who follows her husband on the funeral pyre will find liberation from the endless cycles of death and birth.'

Unmādinī bowed with hands pressed together. She returned home, bathed and prayed. She made large gifts to Brahmins, wandering yogis and the poor. Then she went to the cremation grounds, circumambulated the pyre where her husband's body burned and prayed: 'O Lord, I am your servant now and in every lifetime to follow.' She walked into the centre of the burning pyre and was consumed.

The Vetāla fell silent. There was the sound of the king's feet tramping through dry leaves and wild dogs howling far off. The corpse-demon whispered: 'O Wise Judge, tell me: in this story, whose virtue was the greatest?'

'The king's,' Vikramāditya replied. 'For in this world, the seasons follow the sun and tides follow the moon. In all places and times, the low follows the high. Thus, it is proper for servants to give up their lives for the masters and for wives to sacrifice themselves for their husbands. These are not extraordinary deeds. The king, however, could have justly claimed Unmādinī as his, but did not. His virtue was beyond that was expected and he died as a result.'

STORY 17

Unchanging

When the Vetāla spoke, the outer world faded and the stories grew real. At each tale's conclusion, King Vikrāmaditya knew he would be required to make judgements, as if he ruled in these storylands. Then, briefly, the storytelling would end, and the outer world return, ever less substantial. But the demon's stories never stopped for long. One tale led to another, with only a slight pause in which the king was, for a moment, walking through the dark forest with his weightless burden.

O Majesty, once in the city of Ujjayinī, when wise King Mahāsena built the turquoise-tiled temple, there lived a virtuous and wealthy Brahmin named Devaśarma. Despite his great virtues, his only son, Gunākara, was a compulsive gambler and thief. When he had lost all his own money gambling, he stole from his father, and when he had lost that, he stole jewellery from his fiancée. When, finally, his family could put up with this no longer, they threw him out of the house and onto the street.

Without home, family, money or friends, Gunākara was alone and hungry. He left the city of his birth and wandered for days until he found himself at a charnel ground. There a yogi, his body covered with cow-dung ash, was sitting at the edge of a fire as smoke swirled around him. Gunākara pressed his hands together, bowed to the renunciant and sat on the ground before him.

'O wanderer, are you hungry?' the yogi asked.

'Yes, Holy One, I am,' Gunākara replied.

'Would you eat anything?'

'I will be grateful for whatever you give me.'

The yogi gave the young man a human skull filled with rice. Gunākara was horrified. 'Oh no. I can't eat from a corpse's skull,' he exclaimed.

Holding the skull in both hands, the yogi chanted spells over the rice, and slowly a yakśini, a consort of the God of Wealth, emerged from the steam above the rice. She had golden skin, delicate hands, tiny feet, broad, silk-clad hips, a slender waist and large golden breasts. She swayed like a southern breeze and smiled at the gambler. She stood before the yogi and said: 'O Master, whatever you command, I will do.'

'Give this man all that he secretly desires,' the ascetic said.

The yakśini then rose, spinning in the air, and around her a lavish palace appeared to fill the whole of space. It was surrounded by fountains and gardens and filled with soft divans and sandalwood furniture. Six serving girls smiled invitingly and male slaves waited to attend the wanderer. The yakśini led him by the hand and seated him on a marble stool before an alabaster table. Musicians played languid melodies. Every kind of meat, fish, rice and rare condiment was placed before him, and Gunākara ate without restraint. Then the yakśini rubbed his body with a paste of saffron, sandalwood and rosewater. She dressed him in translucent silk the colour of pearl. She placed a garland of lotus flowers around his neck and led him to the bedroom.

She was arrayed in the same kinds of garments and flowers as he, and the two passed the night enjoying each other's bodies. They glowed with bliss like clouds at sunset.

When morning came, the wandering exile found himself lying on the bare ground in the same dirty clothes he had worn for days. The bed, the silk robes, the perfumed gardens and the yakśini herself had vanished completely. All that remained was the charnel ground, the smoking fire and the yogi. 'Master, O Holy One, what just happened? The yakśini and her dwelling are gone. How can get her back?'

The ascetic replied: 'She came to me because I know the ancient rites and spells she cannot resist.'

'Master, teach me this magic,' Gunākara begged.

The yogi then taught him the mantras and mudras that would achieve his desires. 'Do these practices every night at midnight while sitting in a pool of cold water. Do this for forty days with unwavering concentration.'

Gunākara found a secluded glen with a small deep pool in the forest nearby. There he stayed for six weeks, immersing himself at midnight, reciting mantras and making offerings. Demons came to obstruct him. Turquoise snakes slid into the pool, toads brushed against him, scorpions floated towards him, fish with razor teeth grazed his back, tigers with pale eyes circled the pool and vultures leered at him from nearby trees. He remained steadfast and undeterred. Soon they disappeared. When he had completed this practice, he returned to the yogi. 'Repeat it,' said the ascetic. 'But this time you must sit in a fire.'

'I will do as you command,' said Gunākara, 'but, with your permission, first I will go tell my family what I am doing. They have had no word about me for months, and surely it will ease their minds to see me.'

The yogi let him go with a shrug.

When his father and his family saw him in the robes of a renunciant, they embraced him and wept. 'O my son, where have you been?' his father cried. 'Months ago, you left without a word. We thought you had forgotten us. It is said that one who abandons his family is lower than the lowest. Those who slight their parents are impious and will never, in this life or any other, find liberation. The Great God Brahma has said this.'

To this outburst, Gunākara snapped: 'Have you forgotten that it was you who drove me out of our family home? I do not begrudge you this. I have learned that nothing lasts.

'Who is my father?' Gunākara went on. 'Who is my mother or wife or brother? You are all merely atoms temporarily joined, and inevitably these will separate. That is the fate of all things. Clinging to family is no more useful than worshipping clay idols. I will practise meditation and nothing else.'

Having said this, he returned to the forest and found a bleak secluded spot where for forty days and nights he sat amid a bonfire, saying mantras and making offerings. And yet, when he was finished, the yakśini did not appear to him. He went to the yogi and told him that all his practices had no results.

At this point the Vetāla stopped. 'Why, O King,' it asked. 'Why did Gunākara have no success?'

The answer emerged of its own accord: 'Because Gunākara's mind was divided between the world he had left and the world to which he aspired; he accomplished nothing. Only one who gives his entire being to his goal can accomplish it.'

STORY 18

Three Fathers

King Vikramāditya and the Vetāla were again returning to the charnel ground, and again, the corpse-demon was telling a story.

Your Majesty, perhaps you have heard of Sundara, a king of immense wealth who ruled the yellow-walled Kankolam? Well, in that city during his reign there lived Dhanakśaya, a prosperous merchant, and his daughter, Dhanavatī. When she was a child, her father promised her in marriage to his close friend, Gaurīdatta, also a wealthy merchant. After she became a woman, she went to live with him and soon had a daughter, Mohini. But her husband died ten years later, and his kinfolk seized his house and wealth, leaving Dhanavatī destitute. She had been the mistress but was now a servant. Finally, late one night, she set out with her daughter to return to her parents' house.

Dhanavatī had not visited her family since childhood and soon was lost. She found herself in a vast charnel ground. In the dark, her foot struck a thief impaled on a pillar driven into the earth. He cried out in agony: 'Who is so cruel as to inflict more pain on me?'

'Forgive me,' she said, 'I didn't mean to hurt you.'

The thief responded in a remarkably reasonable voice: 'Whether one gives pain or pleasure, it is entirely in the hands of fate. We make plans but no one knows what determines the outcome. Life rarely turns out as we hoped.'

Dhanavatī was shocked. 'Who are you,' she asked, 'who suffers so terribly, yet speaks so well?'

The thief replied: 'I have read many texts, but I am still a convicted thief. For three days I have lain here, yet my life has not yet left this body.'

'How did this happen to you?' she asked.

Rather than answer, the thief said: 'I am not married, but even now I desire a son so that my passage on the earth will not be forgotten nor entirely despised. If you promise me your daughter in marriage, I will give you ten million gold coins.' Dhanavatī thought carefully. She had no money; by promising her daughter to the thief, both could be happy. She asked the thief: 'Even if I agree that my daughter will marry you and give you a son, how can this happen? You are about to die. She is still a child.'

The thief replied: 'Perform a marriage ceremony for us now. When she is capable of childbearing, find a handsome young Brahmin. Give him five hundred gold coins. Have them sleep together. Soon, she will have my son.'

Dhanavatī performed a simple marriage ceremony by having her daughter walk four times around the impaling stake and the dying thief. Then the thief whispered to her: 'There is a well with stone walls directly east of here. Next to it is a banyan tree with six main branches. Where the longest branch emerges from the tree, dig down two feet and you will find the gold coins. They are yours.' Then the thief gasped, exhaled sharply and died.

Dhanavatī went directly east and found the well and the banyan tree. She dug down until she found five large clay pots. She opened one and saw it was filled with gold. She took a few coins and carefully refilled the hole. She found the way to her parents' house and told them everything. They helped her retrieve the great treasure and brought it home.

Dhavanavatī bought a large parcel of land, built a large fine house and lived there while her daughter grew up. Mohini grew to become an alluring woman. She and her attendant often looked at the passersby on the road before their house. One day, Mohini happened to see a handsome young Brahmin; their eyes met and, as if pierced by a single arrow shot from the bow of Kāma, God of Desire, they fell in love. Mohini said to her companion: 'Have this man present himself to my mother. Tell her I am in love.'

The companion hurried after the Brahmin and brought him to Mohini's mother, who looked at him carefully. She saw that this was the man the thief had foretold. 'O Brahmin,' she said, 'my daughter is young and lovely. I will give you five hundred gold coins to father her son.' He was happy to accept.

The lavender light of evening descended. Dhanavatī instructed her servants to provide the young Brahmin with the eight kinds of pleasure: perfume, clothing, ornamentation, music, food, spices, a woman, sex. Dhanavatī wished her daughter's lover to enjoy all of these. Darkness fell and a half-moon rose; the young Brahmin was taken to the bridal chamber. All through the night, Mohini and he never slept; they enjoyed every delight that two bodies together may. In the morning, he left.

Mohini's friends were full of questions: 'Tell us! What did you and your lover do?'

Mohini replied: 'He touched my lips with the tip of his fingers. I lost all consciousness of being myself.' On that very night, Mohini conceived a child.

Nine months later, Mohini gave birth to a boy, and six nights afterwards, she had a dream. She saw an ascetic: his body was covered with the white ashes of burnt cow dung; his hair was white; a white crescent moon shone on his forehead. He wore a white Brahminical thread and two necklaces, one of skulls, the other of writhing white snakes. He sat on a white lotus with a trident in one hand and a skull cup in the other. He gazed at Mohini and said: 'Tomorrow at midnight, place a bag of one thousand gold coins in a large covered basket. On top of the coins, place your son. Close the basket and leave it at the gate of the king's palace.'

Mohini ran and told her mother about this vision. Mother and daughter agreed that they must do what the ascetic demanded. That very day, they placed the gold and the baby in a basket and left it at the palace gate.

On the same night that Mohini had her vision, the king also had a dream. He saw a black wrathful deity with five heads, each wearing a white crescent moon on his forehead and each with three bloodshot eyes, a wide leering mouth and steel razor-sharp teeth. Its body had ten arms; five held tridents and five held skull cups of blood. The deity's words echoed in the king's head without any audible speech. 'O King, today you will find, at your palace gate, a basket. Inside you will find a male child sleeping on top of a sack of gold coins. Raise this child as your own, O King. It is he who will maintain your kingdom.'

The king woke suddenly and went to the queen. He told her about his vision, then hurried to the gate. Just as the deity had promised, there was a large basket and within it, a child lying on a sack of gold. He had servants bring the basket to his throne room and called for holy men and astrologers to inspect the child. 'What kind of marks of royalty or distinction do you find on this child?'

The sages looked at the baby, then spoke: 'O Great King, there are three marks on this child that point to his fate: a broad chest, a high forehead and large features. Additionally, he has thirty-two auspicious marks. Your Majesty, we must tell you how rare this is. Most men have only three or four. You need not fear for the future of your realm. This child will rule the kingdom well.'

The king was pleased and gave all the sages pearl necklaces. He then asked them to choose a name for the boy. They said to him: 'First, sit on the throne together with your queen with the child on her lap. Then summon musicians, singers and dancers. Provide food and drink for everyone and let the celebration last for two days. Then we will give the boy a name.'

The king summoned his ministers and stewards and commanded them to do as the sages advised. The king and queen sat side by side with the boy on her lap. Their throne was placed on a raised square platform at the centre of a mandala of rice, dyed in the colours of the four directions and adorned with bowls of meat, sweetmeats and fruit, as well as jars of perfume. Brahmins and sages chanted. Astrologers determined that that the boy should be called Haridatta. He was from that moment on his father's heir.

By the age of nine, he had learned the Vedas and by fourteen, he had mastered the sciences and all martial arts. He was both an inspired poet and a great scholar. Two years later, fate brought an end to both his parents' lives. He then became king of Kankolam. He ruled justly and well.

When Haridatta's kingdom was secure, his mind turned to less material concerns. He thought: 'Many were responsible for my existence and good fortune. I owe all my good fortune to three men: a thief, the young Brahmin and my adoptive father, the king. What have I done for them? What can I do to aid them through the endless cycles of birth and death?'

Contemplating these things, King Haridatta decided to perform extensive funeral offerings to his forbears. He went to Gāyā and, by the sacred River Phalgu, he called out the names of his three fathers. He was about to offer sacred food, perfume and wine when suddenly, three hands rose from the water to receive the offering. King Haridatta recognized whose hands they were, but he could not decide to which one he should give the first offering.

The corpse-demon stopped. 'And now, O Wise King, to whom should King Haridatta make the principal offering?'

The answer rose unbidden in King Vikramāditya's mind: 'The thief!'

'And why?'

King Vikramāditya answered: 'The seed of the Brahmin who fathered him was bought and paid for. The king accepted a thousand gold coins to raise and educate the boy. Thus, both were paid for their services. Neither has a right to any offering at all.'

With that, in the blink of an eye, the King Vikramāditya found himself again beginning his journey with the cold vapour of the Vetāla around his shoulder.

STORY 19

Love and Ruling II

'King Vikramāditya, listen,' the Vetāla whispered, paused, then began.

King Rūpasena, a lustful man and avid hunter, ruled Ćitrakūtam, a city famed even now for ruby-red sunsets. One day, he went hunting alone in an unfamiliar forest and lost his way. He found himself in a lush park with a tiled pool and small temple at its centre. Emerald hummingbirds and yellow finches swooped amid flowerbeds at the forest's edge. The king was suddenly exhausted, tied his horse to a tree branch, lay down in the cool shade and slept. When he opened his eyes, he thought he was dreaming.

A dark slender girl of unearthly delicacy was picking flowers nearby. Spellbound, he watched as she walked in his direction. She hadn't seen him and froze when he stood suddenly and addressed her: 'Beautiful you are, but don't you think you should greet a visitor to your temple grounds?'

Startled, the girl didn't know what to say. The king came closer. 'All guests, whether thieves or kings, should be received with respect and honour.'

The girl remained silent. She stared at the imposing stranger, and he stared back. Passion seized them; both were overwhelmed and could not move.

They did not notice a tall Brahmin yogi, the girl's father, emerging from the forest and approaching them. The yogi recognized the king and saw at once that he and his daughter had fallen in love. When the king noticed the holy man, he turned from the girl and tried to hide his feelings by asking for a blessing. The yogi held his hand over him, intoning: 'Sire, may Viśnu and all his avatars grant you a long and prosperous life.'

Then he asked: 'O King, what brought you to this place?'

The king replied: 'Holy One, I came to hunt.'

'And why,' the yogi asked. 'Why do you insist on committing such a sin? Don't you care that what you call pleasure brings terror and suffering to many others other beings?'

The king bowed and put his hands together. 'Instruct me.'

The Brahmin replied: 'Listen, sire. When a man kills a bird or animal, he commits a great sin by harming and killing them. He will suffer equally in his later rebirths. But when he cherishes such beasts and birds and cares for them, he earns merit that will follow him from life to life. No spiritual austerities equal the virtue of compassion; no happiness equals that of peacefulness; no wealth equals that of friendship; and no virtue is the equal of mercy.'

King Rūpasena bowed. 'O Wise Brahmin, I cannot undo what has been done. The many sins I committed were the result of my ignorance. But now, with your guidance, I promise I will sin no more.'

The yogi was pleased and said: 'Your remorse and your vow have moved me deeply. If there is anything in my power to grant you, ask for it.'

The king did not hesitate. 'O Holy One, give me this woman in marriage.'

The yogi agreed. Taking his daughter's hand, he gave her to the king. He walked around the couple four times, and thus they were married. The king swung the yogi's daughter up onto his horse behind him and they set off for his palace. When the moon rose, the king stopped, spread a blanket on the ground and lay down with his wife.

That midnight, a Brahmarakśasa, a pale-yellow Brahmin-devouring demon, crashed out of the trees, pounced on the king and snarled: 'No, King, you I cannot eat. You are from the Kśatriya caste. But ...' It sniffed the king's bride '... her, a Brahmin woman, I can eat.'

'No,' the king cried. 'Don't do this, I beg you. We have just married and only begun to share the pleasures of love. Leave her. I will grant whatever you request.'

The iron-toothed demon replied: 'O Ruler over Men, I will spare your wife if, in one week, you hand me the freshly severed head of a seven-year-old Brahmin boy.'

The king quickly agreed: 'It shall be as you wish.'

The next morning the king returned to his palace and told his minister about his new wife, the demon and his promise. 'Do not worry, sire,' the minister replied, 'I know what to do.'

The minister took two pounds of gold and several bags of gems to a goldsmith and paid the man double his fee to complete a jewel-studded gold image of Viśnu in one day. When the statue was completed, he placed it on a red-and-gold cart in the capital's main square. Eight soldiers guarded the idol. 'When people stop to stare,' he ordered, 'tell them the statue will belong to a Brahmin with a seven-year-old son if he allows the king to cut off his son's head.'

Many came to look at the gold statue, but only on the third day did a poor and dissolute Brahmin consider the offer. He told his wife: 'This is an opportunity for us. We have three sons: nine, seven and five years old. If we sacrifice the seven-year-old, we will have two left and all the wealth we need besides.'

His wife replied: 'I couldn't bear to let our youngest be killed.'

'Nor could I let the eldest die,' said the father. 'But the seven-year-old ...' he continued, 'If one is poor, why be born?'

Then the second son spoke up: 'Father, if my death makes your life and the life of my brothers happy, I will sacrifice myself for you.'

The Brahmin then took his seven-year-old son to the royal palace, gave him to the guards and took the jewelled idol home.

The guards brought the boy to the minister, who cared for him until, on the seventh day, amid clouds of foul-smelling orange smoke, the pale-yellow iron-toothed Brahmarakśasa burst into the throne room and demanded that the king fulfil his vow. As politely as if he were receiving a well-born supplicant, the king had the demon seated on a gold chair and served a crystal goblet of wine. The demon shook his head and hissed. The king nodded and summoned the boy, unsheathed his sword and prepared to behead him. The boy looked at the monarch; first he laughed, then he cried. The king's sword descended like a lightning bolt and cut through the boy's neck; his head flew across the room and rolled to the demon's feet.

When the Brahmin yogi, the father of the king's bride, heard of this, he realized that he had been deceived by an immoral king.

He thought to himself: 'Possessions may satisfy your desires, but clinging blindly to your cravings makes the world into hell.'

At this point, the corpse-demon stopped. He asked: 'Now, O Royal King, why did the child, at the moment of his death, laugh?'

The king answered: 'The boy laughed because he thought: "A mother protects her child; a father cherishes his son; and a king nurtures his subjects. But my parents have surrendered me to a king who, sword drawn, is ready to end my life to satisfy his lust. I am lucky to leave such an evil world." That is why he laughed.'

'And if so,' the Vetāla continued, 'why did he then cry?'

'O Vetāla,' replied the king. 'The boy cried because, as he looked around, he saw that no one felt the slightest flicker of pity for him.'

With that the Vetāla was gone, and the king was alone in the barren forest. He then turned back and soon again he had climbed the dead tree. Now the cold mist of the corpse-spirit shifted lightly on his shoulders and back, then its clammy whisper was again insinuating itself inside his ear. The painful tedium of the king's labours dissolved within the reality of another tale.

STORY 20

Fate and Love

O King, a very rich merchant, Arthadatta, and his daughter, Anangamanjarī, lived in the green-walled city of Viśāla, when Vipulaśekhara was the envious royal ruler there. While she was still a child, Arthadatta had his daughter married to a merchant friend's young son, Maninābha. A few days after the marriage, Maninābha left as an apprentice on a trading voyage that would last for many years. While he was away, Anangamanjarī blossomed into womanhood.

One day, as she gazed down from the roof of her father's house on the crowds passing below, she saw a handsome young Brahmin, Kamalākara. At that moment, he happened to look up and their eyes met. A blazing arrow of passion shot through both their hearts at once. Kamalākara almost lost consciousness. He wandered in a daze until he reached a friend's house and he fell into a faint. As Anangamanjarī watched him walk away, she felt a yawning void, the loss of one she craved more than life, and everything around her dissolved. Her attendant found her lying senseless in the sun and sprinkled rosewater to revive her. The young girl's eyes fluttered as she woke. 'Ah, ah,' she cried out as if in the throes of making love. 'O Kāmadeva, God of Desire, you have pierced me to the core. Why do you inflict such pain on me, a woman so innocent and weak?'

She stayed on the roof and as the moon rose, she wept: 'O Moon, the poets say your gentle silver light restores all it touches. Not so. It burns like cobra's venom in my veins.'

She turned to her companion in desperation: 'The moon is burning me to death.'

Her companion was afraid and helped her inside. 'Aren't you ashamed of yourself?' she whispered to the girl. 'You mustn't talk like this.'

Anangamanjari shook her head violently. 'I can't stop. Kāmadeva has made me without shame.'

The attendant realized that her young mistress had been seized by love and she took this seriously. She said: 'I will make sure your suffering is relieved.' And she hurried off to find the man with whom her mistress had become infatuated.

But, left alone, the young girl could not believe that the agony of her longing would ever be eased. She wanted to die; perhaps she would find her lover in another life. Mad with desire, she made a noose from a silk cord, put it around her neck and tossed the other end over a ceiling beam. She was about to hang herself when her attendant returned and pulled the noose from the girl's neck.

'More can be accomplished by the living than the dead,' the woman told her. 'Lie down and sleep. The young Brahmin you love is named Kamalākara. I know where he lives and will bring him to you right away.'

The attendant rushed through the moonlit night to find Kamalākara's gates open. He was lying on a couch in the courtyard, as devastated by longing as Anangamanjarī. He writhed in anguish as a friend rubbed him with sandalwood oil and fanned him with a plantain leaf in a vain effort to ease his suffering. He was moaning, 'Love is burning me. My nerves are on fire. Bring me poison. End this agony.'

The girl's companion entered the courtyard and said to Kamalạ̄kara: 'I come from the one you love. She suffers as you do. Come to her now and your pain will be transformed to bliss.'

The two then raced to the house where Anangamanjarī waited. They ran, but when they arrived, the girl was lying on the floor, dead. The young man emitted a terrible scream of anguish and he too died.

Next morning, when the sun rose, servants and attendants took the two lovers' bodies to the cremation ground and set them together on the top of a funeral pyre. At this very moment, Anangamanjarī's husband, who had just returned from years of trading voyages, passed by the cremation ground. He heard the terrible wailing and, though he had not seen his child bride for years, he recognized her, lying atop a burning pyre beside a strange man. He had longed for her throughout his travels so, when someone in the crowd told him what had led to this tragedy, he was overcome with grief. He threw himself into the fire and was consumed. All the people of the city, even the king, shook their heads and grieved when they heard this story.'

The Vetāla paused. 'Tell me, O Great Vikramāditya, of these three, whose love do you think was the greatest?'

The king replied without thinking, 'The husband, he had the deepest love.'

'And why?' hissed the corpse-demon.

King Vikramāditya replied: 'He, who had not seen his wife for many years, on seeing her dead from love for another, put aside anger, bitterness and regret. He followed his love for her into the fire and gave up his life. This is a deeper love than the sudden passion that consumed the other two.'

'Just so,' said the demon and was gone.

STORY 21

A Corpse Revived

Again, the chilly whisper echoed in King Vikramāditya's ear, and again, he was absorbed in yet another tale.

In a small white-gated city named Jayasthala, during the reign of its easy-going king, Vīramardana, there lived a wise and virtuous Brahmin, Viśnusvāmī. Unfortunately, Viśnusvāmī's first son was a gambler, the second a lover of prostitutes, the third dallied with loose women and the fourth was an atheist.

For years, the Brahmin endured their many sins and follies in silence, but one day he could bear it no longer. He had them stand before him and raged. First, he berated his eldest son. 'Fool! In every book of law it says: "Cut off the nose and ears of anyone who gambles. Expel him from wherever he lives so he cannot influence others."'

The gambling son was shocked, but the old man continued, 'Everyone knows that wealth never stays in a gambler's house. He has no morals. Even if he is a householder with a wife and children, he should be cast out. Luck is the only thing he believes in.'

Then he turned to the two middle sons: 'As for you two, you are only attracted to the easy seductions of courtesans and are constantly influenced by the schemes of whores. For years, they've been taking your money. You are idiots to fall for such women; you are surrendering your decency, honesty, judgement and morality. For momentary pleasures, you let your souls wither and your minds rot. You think you seek love? You are loved in the same way a beggar loves a wallet left in the street.'

And here he turned to the atheist: 'You are unable to see beyond the boundaries of a single life. Nothing matters but what you think you know or what you think you can obtain. You are a self-deceived know-it-all, consumed by pride.'

The Brahmin raged on: 'None of you learned anything as children. Now you are men and your lives are lost in delusion. Your past provided no guidance and your future gives you nothing to rely on.'

The Brahmin's sons were deeply shocked to hear their father speak this way. They decided that they must change the way they lived. They knew they would one day need to support themselves, so they decided to learn occult lore and magic. They went to a distant city where their reputations were not known and, for several years, applied themselves diligently to these studies. When they had become sufficiently accomplished, they decided to return home. They had mastered many disciplines, rituals and incantations, could tell the future, make love potions, cure diseases, divine for wells and curse enemies. But they were most proud to have learned the rites and spells needed to revive a dismembered corpse. They had seen this done several times but had yet to do it themselves. They were sure that when their father saw them perform this miracle, he would be proud of them.

During their journey home, they encountered a hunter skinning and dismembering a dead tiger. They watched him take the skeleton apart and place the bones, along with the butchered meat, in the skin, and sling the skin and bones over his shoulder. 'We don't want to make fools of ourselves in front of our father,' the brothers agreed. 'We should practise our spells and revive this tiger.'

They bought the hunter's tiger skin, flesh and bones, and when he was out of sight, they began the rituals to resurrect it. The first son put the bones on the unrolled skin, sprinkled secret substances and chanted incantations. Suddenly, the bones came together, and the skeleton stood immobile. The second son placed the flesh on the skeleton and fixed them there with substances and spells. The flayed tiger now seemed capable of movement. The third son used different spells to fix the skin to the body. The brothers were pleased that it seemed they were looking at a tiger poised to spring. Then the fourth brother, the one-time atheist, again using the methods they all had learned, chanted spells and sprinkled holy water on the tiger. Immediately it came fully and completely to life. It sprang on the four brothers and, in a frenzy, claws and teeth flashing, it ripped them apart and devoured them.

The corpse-spirit snickered. 'Tell me now, O Wise King, which of these four stupid men was the stupidest?'

King Vikramāditya did not need to think to reply: 'The fourth idiot who brought the tiger back to life was obviously the biggest fool. You didn't need me to answer that.'

Again, King Vikramāditya was alone and again he was starting his journey with the Vetāla on his back.

STORY 22

Transferring Consciousness

'Once there was a Brahmin Yogi named Nārāyana,' the Vetāla began, as if this were the first story he had ever told.

He lived in Viśvapuram, a city known for its deep blue cloudless skies. This was in the fortunate time when the renowned Scholar-King Vidaghda ruled. One day, as Nārāyana napped in the shade of a banyan tree, he reflected: 'I am now old, and my body is worn out. Every moment brings pain, and every desire brings frustration. It really would be wonderful to enjoy life again.' As he dozed, he mused, 'Is it necessary for me to suffer so? Years ago, I learned a secret method of exchanging my body for the body of another. Now is the perfect time to leave this failing carcass and enter the body of a strong young man.'

Nārāyana wandered the streets and markets to find a young man whose body he could make his own. After three months, as he felt death stalking him, Nārāyana encountered a vigorous and intelligent young Brahmin. As they sipped tea together, the aging Brahmin learned that the young man's parents had just died. He had no relatives nor close friends and lived alone in a house on the edge of the forest. 'No one,' the yogi thought, 'would notice if he seemed different.' The old man wept and laughed to realize he had found his next body.

'Several evenings later, he went to an empty field adjoining the young Brahmin's garden wall. He sat cross legged as he performed recitations and offerings. Slowly his consciousness rose from his body. It floated up through the night air, swept the over wall and, like the lightest perfume, entered the young man's bedroom window. He settled softly on the pillow next to the young man who sighed gently in the depth of sleep. Then, in an almost inaudible whisper, the aged spirit recounted everything important in his past: the things he had done, the people he had known, the texts and rites he had studied, the yearnings he still longed to fulfil. In the field outside, the body he was leaving slowly deflated as story after story, recounting every accomplishment, love, unrequited passion, every loss and every triumph entered the sleeping young man.

This recitation continued through night, the next day and all the next night after that. The old Brahmin entered a splendid young body and took possession of it entirely. It was like putting on a new silk shirt. When the process was done, the old body fell to the ground. It was nothing but an empty sack of wrinkled skin. The young Brahmin's consciousness was lost, confused, and scattered in the dark. Then, in his new form, Natāyāna returned home. By his manner of speech and his ways of acting, his kinsfolk soon recognized him in this new form. They guessed what he had done. 'Now, in this new body,' he said, 'I am again a wanderer.' Then he told his astonished and uneasy relatives: 'Our life is illusion. Believing that consciousness ends is a great illusion. No strand in our awareness ever breaks; it just becomes invisible.

Somewhere else, in the vast weaving of time, it will be visible again.' With this, the Brahmin Nārāyana, in his new and youthful body, announced: 'For me, what is there to do but wander on as a pilgrim in a dream.' And so, he departed.

Then the corpse-spirit hissed: 'Now, O King, when this Brahmin found a new body, why first did he weep, then laugh?'

The pain in the king's head forced him to speak. 'The Brahmin recalled how much his mother loved him when he was a baby. He remembered how much he enjoyed his father's guidance as a young man. He remembered how much he had enjoyed being in the body he was about to leave, so he wept. Then, because he found a youthful body in which he could fulfil his longings, he laughed.'

Then the Vetāla was gone, the king was walking, climbing a tree, and in a now-familiar blur, he was listening to another story.

STORY 23

Sensitivity II

O Kindly Monarch, when the vain King Dharmadvaja ruled in Dharmadpuram, a city famed for its saffron market, there lived a Brahmin, Govinda, learned in the Vedas and conscientious in fulfilling his spiritual obligations. His four sons, Haridatta, Somadatta, Yajnadatta and Brahmadatta were all intelligent, scholarly and obedient. One day the eldest son, Haridatta, became violently ill and died. Govinda was so completely broken by grief that it seemed he too would soon die.

Viśnu Śarma, the royal priest, came to council Govinda at his bedside. 'O Learned One,' he said, 'you well know that this world is a fountain of unending sorrows. Here we all suffer from sickness, old age and death. We suffer from innumerable kinds of loss. We suffer simply because we cannot escape suffering. You must know it is foolish to agonize over things you cannot avoid. O Govinda, it is far better to cultivate wisdom and understanding, to meditate, to pray for others, than it is to grieve and weep.'

Govinda accepted the priest's advice. He decided to devote the rest of his life to meditation and the welfare of others. He told his sons of his intention, then asked, 'I wish to mark the beginning of my new life by sacrificing a turtle. Get me the largest and most beautiful sea turtle you can find.'

The sons went to the harbour and gave a fisherman three silver coins for an exceptionally large, rare green-and-yellow sea turtle. Somadatta was about to pick it up, but suddenly stopped. 'Oh,' he said in disgust, 'the smell will stay in my hair and cling to my pillows and spoil my sleep.'

He told Yajnadatta to take it. But he in turn said: 'I cannot. The smell will stay on my skin and be repulsive when I am making love to my wives.'

He instructed the youngest, Brahmadatta, to carry the turtle. He too refused, saying: 'Certainly not. It will leave a slight fishy smell on my hands that will ruin my appetite when I eat.'

None would agree to carry the turtle home and their argument grew increasingly heated. They shouted at each other, cursed and were about to come to blows. The fisherman felt obliged to intervene and urged them to ask the king to resolve their dispute. They left the turtle on the dock and made their way to the palace. They told the king about their father and his wish to sacrifice a turtle and described the sensitivities that made completing this task impossible. The king responded: 'Before I decide, I must test each of you.'

To test the youngest son, the king instructed the royal chef to make a most refined and succulent meal. A private dining room was prepared, and the son was seated before a sumptuous array of delicious dishes. He was about to take his first bite when suddenly he smelled something offensive. He washed his hands five times, left the room and returned to the king.

'Did you enjoy the feast?' asked the king.

The young Brahmin bowed. 'Your Majesty, I could not eat a thing.'

'And why?' asked the king.

'As I said, I am exceptionally sensitive. I could tell that the rice had been grown near a cremation ground. The smell of burning corpses lingered in each grain. This made it impossible to eat a bite.'

The king summoned his chef. 'Where did the rice come from?' he demanded. 'Summon the owner of the rice field.'

And when the owner arrived the king asked: 'Was there a cremation ground near the land where this rice was grown?'

'Yes, Your Majesty,' the man answered, 'it is so.'

When the king heard this, he turned to the youngest son. 'At least where food is concerned, you are a most sensitive man.'

Next, the king sent for the son who enjoyed women. He had a lavish bedroom prepared and called on the city's most reliable procuress to provide the most beautiful and refined courtesan in the kingdom. The king hid behind a screen and watched as the two chatted and joked seductively. Then the young Brahmin began to run his hands over her body. He leaned closer and kissed her, but suddenly pulled away. Though she stroked his neck and cheek, he refused to respond.

The next morning the king sent for him and asked: 'Young sire, did the courtesan I provided please you?'

'No, Your Majesty,' the young man replied. 'I regret to say I found no pleasure with her.'

'And why was that?' the king continued.

'Sire, she was incomparably amusing and beautiful, but when I kissed her, the smell of goat went from her mouth into mine, and all desire ended then and there,' the Brahmin explained.

The king then summoned the procuress and asked: 'Where did you get this woman? On what kind of food was she raised?'

The old woman answered: 'She is my sister's daughter. My sister died when the child was three months old. I brought her up myself, but I had no breast milk with which to feed her and so I brought her up on goat's milk.'

On hearing this, the king turned to the young Brahmin. 'A least when it comes to women, you are indeed extraordinarily sensitive.'

The king then tested Somadatta. He had a bed of silk cushions and satin sheets prepared and placed in a luxurious, soundproofed bedroom. He asked the young Brahmin to spend the night there and, in the morning, asked him: 'Did you sleep comfortably throughout the night?'

'Alas, sire, I couldn't sleep, even for a second,' the Brahmin replied.

'How could this be? I made sure that no sound would disturb you, and that your bed was incomparably comfortable,' the king exclaimed.

'Your Majesty, in the seventh fold of the bedding there was an eyelash. It pricked my back and thus I could not rest, much less sleep.'

On hearing this, the king had his servants examine the bedding and there was, in the seventh fold of the silk sheet, a tiny hair.

'Astounding,' said the king. 'You are indeed, when it comes to bedding, a most sensitive man.'

☠

At this point the corpse-demon stopped. The king walked on for a while, wondering if the story would resume. 'Now, O Wise

King …' The chilly voice brought King Vikrāmaditya back from his wandering thoughts. 'Perhaps you can tell me this. Of these three sensitive young men, who was the most sensitive of all?'

The king knew the answer instantly. 'Certainly, the young Brahmin who found a small hair hidden in his bedding was the most sensitive. The other two had more direct contact with whatever annoyed them.'

When the demon heard this, he was already hanging from his tree, and Vikramāditya was again returning to carry him.

STORY 24

A Corpse Revived II

The Vetāla was again whispering in King Vikramāditya's ear and another story was enfolding him. It was disorienting and oddly comforting.

O Great King, once in the country of the red-faced Kalinga, in the prosperous city of Yajnasthala, lived a great Brahmin scholar named Yajnasoma and his beautiful wife, Somadattā. They were childless, and the Brahmin made many offerings and prayers so that they might have a son. Finally, Somadattā gave birth to a boy who was as beautiful a child as anyone had ever seen. They named him Brahmāsvāmī. When the boy was five, his father began teaching him the śastras. In seven years, the boy had both memorized and comprehended the meaning of all these texts. His learning equalled that of many great scholars, and he was able to serve his father and assist him in his work.

When the boy was fifteen, he caught pneumonia and died. The Brahmin and his wife were distraught; they wept and could not eat or drink. All the Brahmin's closest relatives and friends gathered to escort the boy to the cremation grounds. Everyone was saying:

'Look! Even in death, Brahmāsvāmī remains as beautiful as if he were alive!'

An old yogi happened to be sitting next to the road as they passed by. He couldn't help hearing them and began thinking: 'My body is old, painful, worn out. I can't continue much longer. If I transfer my consciousness into this boy's body, I can meditate comfortably for many more years.'

The yogi followed the procession to the cremation ground, and when the body had been placed on the pyre, he moved close to the dead boy's corpse. He began whispering intently in its ear. Brahmāsvāmī's parents and friends were grateful that a venerable holy man was spending so much time blessing the boy, but the yogi was transferring his consciousness into the boy by whispering chants and telling stories of the events and deeds that had shaped his life. He focused all his awareness and with a sound like a bubble popping, projected himself out into the boy's body. For the yogi, it felt like slipping into a freshly made bed.

Then he turned his head back and forth, looking from side to side, and spoke the names of Rāma and Kriśna over and over. He sat up and rubbed his eyes as if waking from a night's sleep.

Brahmāsvāmī's parents and family were astonished and elated. They lifted the boy from the pyre and rejoicing, brought him home. But as they left the cremation ground, Yajnasoma, the boy's father, noticed the shrivelled corpse of the old yogi lying on the ground. Immediately he understood what had happened. He burst out laughing and then he wept.

'Now, O Wise King, once again, please tell me this,' the Vetāla murmured. 'Why did the Brahmin laugh, and then why did he cry?'

The question was familiar and the king promptly replied. 'The Brahmin laughed when he saw that the yogi had taken his son's body because he realized that he too could perfect such an art and need never die. But then he thought: "The day will come when time will force me to abandon this body of mine and with it all who are dear to me." And thus, he wept.'

The Vetāla wriggled. 'Ah My King, that's as good an answer as before,' he said and vanished.

STORY 25

A Question with No Answer

Again, King Vikramāditya was striding through a dark and clammy forest with the mist-like presence draped around his shoulders. And from the mist, a familiar whisper.

Now, O King, here's another tale, perhaps for you, the best of all. It took place in the south, in Dharmadpuram, a city known for its jade-green walls whose ruler at the time was Mahābala, a brave, energetic but unlucky king.

It happened that the king of the neighbouring Bhil tribe assembled a vast army and besieged Dharmadpuram. Mahābala's small army managed to hold out for three days, but the situation became hopeless and many of his soldiers turned against him and opened the city gates. Those loyal to Mahābala were decimated. He had no allies, so when night fell, he fled with his wife and daughter into the jungle. They made their way through overgrown trails and at dawn found themselves on the outskirts of a large village. Leaving the queen and princess in a dense grove of Sal trees, the king went to find food and water. He approached the village cautiously, but a large contingent of heavily armed Bhils saw him, and he was quickly surrounded.

For almost three hours, King Mahābala fought to keep them at bay. But finally, an arrow struck him in the forehead and stunned him. As he reeled back, a Bhil warrior ran forward and cut off his head.

Hearing the shouts and clanging of battle, the queen and princess had crawled through the undergrowth to watch. When they saw King Mahābala killed, they thought they would themselves die of horror and grief. But they stifled their sorrow and crept deeper in the jungle. Two days later, they thought they were safe and wept aloud They lay down and clung to each other but could not sleep.

'Without knowing it, the queen and princess had strayed into the nearby domain of King Ćandra Sena. It was late afternoon, and the king and his son were out hunting in the jungle. The king looked down and noticed two sets of footprints. 'Why would two people be walking so deep in the jungle?' he asked the prince who looked, then replied in surprise: 'These are women!'

'Indeed,' the king agreed.

'And sire,' said the prince, 'they were here less than an hour ago.' The king nodded. 'Well, if we find them, the one with longer feet is yours; the other will be mine.'

The son smiled and agreed. Soon they found the queen and princess, lying against a tree trunk, exhausted and distraught.

The two stood up as they heard the king and his son approach. They were relieved to see two men of evident nobility and not the savage tribesman who had just demolished their home and killed their husband and father.

King Ćandra Sena saw that the women were terrified and, to put them at ease, introduced himself and his son. He invited them to stay in his palace and had the princess sit on his horse before him. The prince did the same with the queen. They returned to the royal residence. There, the king took the princess as one of his wives and the prince took the queen as his consort.

A year later, both women gave birth; the princess bore the king a son; her mother, the queen, gave the prince a daughter.

The Vetāla now stopped and asked King Vikramāditya: 'O Perceptive Monarch, O Master of Riddles, tell me this: what then was the relationship between these two children?'

King Vikramāditya thought but could find no answer. It was a chaos of simultaneous possibilities: cousins, nieces, grandchildren. It was the kind of irresolvable confusion that, as he knew, often follows war. There was no untangling it. For once, the king had no answer, and his head did not ache.

Diaspora

The king had fallen into a daze during the continual repetitions of searching for the Vetāla, finding him in the tree, cutting him down, picking him up, walking through the bleak night, listening to another tale and answering a question, again and again, over and over. But now, at this, he was finally speechless. He was shocked by the sudden void.

The corpse-spirit waited, then asked: 'What? You have no answer?'

King Vikrāmditya shook his head and did not speak. Hearing his own footsteps in the forest night, the crackling of leaves, the whirring and faint high squeaking of bats, the distant cries of wild dogs and jackals and something else ... Was his hearing suddenly more acute? The king felt slightly dizzy. The Vetāla's icy voice brought him back to his senses.

'O Worthy King, it is good that finally you can find no more answers. It is good that at last you are silent. Now we near our journey's end, and I will tell you a story that, like a current beneath the waves, caught you long before you were born. Listen carefully. The test to which this story is the key is not a question. It is life and death.

'There is in this very world and time an ash-white demon, the hairs of whose body are like red thorns and whose body itself is like black wood. His powers have enabled him to conquer rulers in the underworld and his ambitions inspire him to defeat kings here on earth. He has come to your city. He has transformed himself into a yogi named Ksāntiśila and you have met him. It is exactly as a demon once told you. It is he who tricked you into accepting twenty-five rubies concealed inside twenty-five mangoes. It is he who has made you undertake this errand of bringing me, a living corpse, to him. Now he sits before a smoking fire in the cremation ground, performing an ancient ritual, chanting mantras, making offerings and preparing to end your life.

'Now, O Patient Vikramāditya, I can no longer draw you into the timeless world of stories. I can no longer make you turn back and start this journey over. I can no longer keep your fate at bay. When you arrive where the demon yogi Ksāntiśila waits, first he will have you throw me into a sacrificial fire. Do this without a second thought. Do not worry on my account. I will, for the first time in aeons, be freed from imprisonment in this lifeless corpse. You cannot imagine how I have longed for this moment.

'Here is my story, O Noble King. Tens of thousands of centuries ago, at the very beginning of this era, I was an ordinary man. I lay with my wife beside the Ganges. I slept and dreamed. This is as vivid to me now as then. I heard twenty-five stories echoing in a dream, and when I woke, I told them to my wife. How was I to know that these tales were part of Śiva's love-play, whispered into Pārvatī's ear, amusements meant for a goddess alone?

'The world was still new, and I was unaware. But ignorance is never a defence. I was cursed by that most powerful of gods.

No matter that I did not deserve such a fate. No matter that my offense was sheer accident. Śiva cursed me to have those stories ever in my mind while I hung from a dead tree in the midst of a haunted forest. There I was imprisoned inside this body as it rotted; dried out like a leather sack; became, over centuries, more and more translucent, more ethereal until it was as you see. I implored the Great One not to leave me in such a state for all eternity. And indeed, he relented. I should be released only if I told these tales to a king as he carried this corpse, back and forth, through the night forest, twenty-five times. I could not imagine that such a thing could ever happen until you came, and we began our journey together. Now this will all be over soon, and this prison of a corpse will be destroyed.

'O Great King Vikramāditya, the twenty-five tales I told have long been the essence of my being. Now they live in you; they are part of your life, and you will carry me into millions of places and times. My existence is inseparable from the story of your life and will continue in whoever hears your history. I will be woven into them. As one tells another, in hundreds of millions of minds, I will become part of hundreds of millions of beings. In aeon after aeon, I will come to life in times and circumstances beyond imagining and without limit. But O Merciful One, my continuing depends on your survival. Your story must not end. You will have to destroy my long-dead body. Throw it in the fire. It is irrelevant.

'But when this corpse is gone, the demon yogi Ksāntiśila will say: "Great King! To complete the work you have promised, now you must prostrate to me with body, speech and mind."

'Noble Vikramāditya, I warn you: if you submit to Ksāntiśila in this way, the moment your chest, eyes, head, knees, feet and hands touch the ground and you surrender your heart and mind, the earth will open beneath you. You will fall into an ocean of burning sulphur. Unending agony will never cease consuming you, repeatedly erasing from human memory. And instantly, the yogi will become the naked power of evil itself and seize the mind of every living being. There will be nothing but chaos, pain and terror. The world will become a cosmic slaughterhouse.'

King Vikramāditya felt the Vetāla quivering on his shoulders and found himself more frightened than he had ever been. 'How can I stop this?' he asked.

'Only by severing the yogi's head from his body; only by making him prostrate to you …' the corpse-demon whispered.

'But how?' the king persisted.

'Like all the other questions you've answered, that can only come from within you. Remember who you are.'

King Vikramāditya had no choice but to walk on, carrying the Vetāla with him, but now the creature's damp presence was heavy and oppressive like a monsoon fog. He had long wished for this journey to reach its end but now, as the king and the Vetāla reached the charnel ground, it felt all too soon. Through the trees, they saw Ksāntiśila, bloodshot eyes glowing, white hair swirling, sitting motionless before a blazing pyre. The king approached and the yogi looked up, smiled, bowed. 'Thank you, Great Majesty, you are an honourable and truthful man. You are a rare being in any age.'

The yogi gestured for the king to approach and pointed to the fire. In a thin metallic voice, he instructed: 'Now, O King, that wretched corpse must be destroyed. Throw it into the flames.'

Quickly, so he would have no second thoughts, King Vikramāditya tossed the feather-light body into the sacrificial fire. The yogi added herbs, perfumes, minerals, wine, flowers, butter to the fire and then all kinds of food, both savoury and sweet. For a while, the Vetāla lay in the flames without catching fire. Then smoke began to rise from the corpse, and suddenly it burst into flames. Roaring filled the air and shook the night sky. The swirling smoke was filled with the cries and whispers of men, women, children and all kind of animals; everywhere there was laughter and shouting, weeping and screaming. The clamour of battle, the cheers of celebrants, the music of ceremonies, the shouts and cries of the marketplace filled the air. The stench was overpowering. Slowly, almost imperceptibly, these diminished into sighs of lovers, sobs of children, groans of the aged, the final exhale of the dying. Then the corpse collapsed in embers, and the echoes of thousands upon thousands of voices dissolved into space.

King Vikramāditya was stunned as his spectral companion vanished, but the yogi Ksāntiśila did not seem to notice and continued chanting as the corpse burned. Only when it was a powdery ash did silence return. Then, in an imperious voice, the yogi said to the king: 'Now complete the task as you promised: prostrate to me, and your glory will be unending. You will have the power to expand your size at will, the power to make your body as light as you wish, the power to make yourself infinitely small, the power to gratify your every desire, the power of having all beings obey you, and the power to subjugate or eliminate all desires whatsoever. All these will be yours.'

King Vikramāditya hesitated. The Vetāla's warning was clear in his mind, but he didn't know what to do. The yogi burst in impatiently, 'Perhaps the idea of prostrating does not please a king, but you gave your word and a king must keep his promises, is this not so?'

Instantly, the king knew how to put an end to the yogi's design. He put his palms together, and with utmost humility, said: 'O Holy One, as you know, I have been a king for a very long time. All the world has bowed at my feet and I have no knowledge of how to make such a prostration myself. I apologize for my ignorance. You are indeed the greatest teacher of this age: can you kindly teach me how to bow down? You must show me how to do this properly.'

The yogi nodded and lowered his hands, knees, chest, shoulders and then his head to the ground. As he did so, King Vikramāditya unsheathed his sword and, with a single stroke, cut through the yogi's neck. For a second, the head did not move.

The yogi's head became a smoking ball with a mouthful of black teeth and orange hair emitting a spray of red flames. It fell to the ground and, of its own accord, rolled in a circle, screaming around the corpse. The body became the headless green spiny lizard, covered with pus and blood, stinking of rotten flesh and excrement. It too burst into bright red flames. King Vikramāditya stood aside and watched through the night until the yogi's physical being had completely consumed itself.

When the sun rose, there was nothing but two patches of scorched earth where the Vetāla and the yogi had once been. King Vikramāditya walked through the smoking charnel ground and returned to his splendid palace and resumed his rule. It seemed to his ministers and servants that he had been gone only a single night. And, just as if there had been no interruption, he continued governing his kingdom wisely and leading his armies well. He listened to all classes of men and women and redressed their grievances. He gave judgements and settled disputes. Legends about King Vikrāmaditya began at once, and were written down in the *Brhatkatha*, the *Kathasaritsagara*, the *Gatha-Saptasati*, the *Vasavadatta*, and in innumerable later texts, dramas, songs and spoken stories, which are current now.

Acknowledgements

This book could not have appeared without Edwin Frank's extraordinary generosity and painstaking care.

All those at NYRB have been similarly gracious and skilled.

Endless thanks to Deborah Marshall, Kidder Smith, Suranjan and Sangeeta Ganguly, Mark Lipovetsky, Tatiana Mihailova, Daniil Lederman and Emilio Ambasz, and John Von Daler, who each have been unstinting in their help and encouragement.

Notes

This retelling of the Vetāla tales was made in reliance on John Platts, *The Baitâl Pachchisi Or, The Twenty-Five Tales of a Sprite*,, Translated from the Hindi Text of Dr Duncan Forbes (One of Her Majesty's Inspectors of Schools in the Central Provinces of India) (Wm. H. Allen & Co., 1871). Release Date: 10 May 2017 [EBook #54697].

The stories are presented here in the same manner and order as in the above edition; the conversations between the Vetāla and King Vikramāditya have been altered.

In addition, I am deeply indebted to Chandra Rajan's superb translation from the Sanskrit of Śivadāsa's *The Five and Twenty Tales of the Genie* (*Vetāla-pañćavinśati*) (Penguin Books India, 1995). Her introduction, commentary and inclusion of tales from other Sanskrit sources are not only profoundly informative but delightful. All proper names in my book have been changed to be in accord with this Sanskrit edition.

Other translations include:

Śivadāsa, *Listen, O King! Five-and-Twenty Tales of Vikram and the Vetal,* adapted and retold by Deepa Agarwal (Puffin Books, 2016).

Captain Sir Richard Burton (tr.), *King Vikram and The Vampire* (Park Street Press, 1992).

Heinrich Zimmer, *The King and The Corpse*, ed. Joseph Campbell (Meridian Books, 1960). This is a commentary on one of the most famous Vetāla tales.

Simhāsana Dvātrimśikā, *Thirty-Two Tales of the Throne of Vikramaditya*, tr. Aditya Narayan Dhairyasheel Haksar (Penguin Books, 1968).

More tales concerning King Vikramāditya

For those interested in renditions of the Vetāla tales in other cultures, please consult:

Rachel Hariette Bust (tr.), *Sagas from the Far East; Or,Kalmouk and Mongolian Traditionary Tales* (Gilbert and Rivington, 1873). Amazon.

About the Author

Douglas J. Penick has published widely and written texts for operas performed at the Munich Biennale and the Santa Fe Opera. The Witter Bynner Foundation supported his three books retelling aspects of the King Gesar epic. His book of essays, *The Age of Waiting*, exploring the sensibility of ecological collapse, came out in 2021 from Arrowsmith Press. In 2025, Punctum Books brought out *Winter Light: On Late Life's Radiance*, an exploration of old age, loss, unexpected discovery and artistic breakthroughs.

HarperCollins *Publishers* India

At HarperCollins India, we believe in telling the best stories and finding the widest readership for our books in every format possible. We started publishing in 1992; a great deal has changed since then, but what has remained constant is the passion with which our authors write their books, the love with which readers receive them, and the sheer joy and excitement that we as publishers feel in being a part of the publishing process.

Over the years, we've had the pleasure of publishing some of the finest writing from the subcontinent and around the world, including several award-winning titles and some of the biggest bestsellers in India's publishing history. But nothing has meant more to us than the fact that millions of people have read the books we published, and that somewhere, a book of ours might have made a difference.

As we look to the future, we go back to that one word—a word which has been a driving force for us all these years.

Read.